THE STORY PIRATES PRESENT

STUCK IN THE STONE AGE

New York Times bestselling author Geoff Rodkey
illustrated by Hatem Aly

COMING SOON:
STORY PIRATES BOOK 2!

An imprint of Rodale Books
733 Third Avenue
New York, NY 10017
Visit us online at RodaleKids.com

Printed in China
Manufactured by RRD Asia 201802
Design by Tom Daly and Jeff Shake
Library of Congress Cataloging-in-Publication Data is on-file with the publisher.
ISBN 978-1-63565-089-1   hardcover
Distributed to the trade by Macmillan
10 9 8 7 6 5 4 3 2 1 hardcover

A BRIEF MESSAGE FROM

ROLO VINCENT

CAPTAIN OF THE STORY PIRATES

Hello, readers! Welcome to the first-ever Story Pirates book!

If you're wondering: "What's a STORY PIRATE...?" we're not actual pirates! We're a motley crew of professional artists, teachers, and comedians who think kids have the BEST ideas. We don't steal treasure—we collect kids' stories and turn them into hilarious books, podcasts, videos, and shows. We even visit schools across the country, helping kids write stories that we perform for them LIVE ON STAGE!

It's amazing fun to help kids bring their stories to life! And that's what this book is all about: we took an idea from one of our audience members, 11-year-old Vince Boberski of Memphis, Tennessee, and turned it into a WHOLE NOVEL!

If you came here to read a great story and nothing else, flip ahead to Chapter 1 and dig in! I promise I won't get mad. I'm a pirate—we're very hard to offend.

Seriously. Flip ahead! Get outta here! It's fine.

If you DIDN'T flip ahead, I have a surprise:

Stuck in the Stone Age isn't just a great story. It can help YOU create great stories of your own!

In the back of this book is the STORY CREATION ZONE, a storytelling how-to guide! As you read the main story, Vince and I will pop up to point out parts of the SCZ that explain how *Stuck in the Stone Age* got built from Vince's idea—and how YOU can build stories of your own!

Want to see how it works? Turn to page 196 to find out.

Did you go? Are you back? Pretty cool, right? If you create any stories of your own using the SCZ, we'd love to see them! Go online (with the help of a parent or guardian) and share them with us at StoryPirates.com!

A BRIEF MESSAGE FROM

VINCE BOBERSKI
KID WRITER

Hi! I'm Vince. I live in Memphis, Tennessee, with my mom and dad, a little sister who gets on my nerves (sometimes), and two dogs named Daisy and Lucy who don't. My favorite sports are running and basketball. My favorite team is the Grizzlies, and my favorite player is Mike Conley. Go Grizz! I like playing saxophone in my school's band and writing stories for school and for fun.

My sister and I listen to the radio on the way to school, and that's where I heard about the Story Pirates contest. It sounded neat, so I sent in my story idea. A LONG time went by, and I kind of forgot about it. One night, my dad told me that we were going on a trip to New York. I had never been, and I was pretty excited.

My dad and I checked into a hotel, and then we walked to a building that looked like it might be a museum. I got suspicious when someone started taking a video of us. When the elevator stopped, we got out (along with the guy following us with a camera), and went into a big glass room. There were a bunch of people in there wearing Story Pirates T-shirts, and they shouted, "Vince, we're turning your story into a book!" Geoff Rodkey, the author, was there, too, and we talked about writing. They even had cookies. It was really exciting!

I like writing because you can write whatever comes to your mind. Even if it doesn't make sense, you can use your imagination to make it make sense. You can rewrite and edit until it's just how you want. Sometimes something really great can come out of it! I never thought that so many people would hear about my idea, and I hope that it will help kids write just for fun.

You are going to have a great time reading what Geoff Rodkey and the Story Pirates have made based on my idea. I hope it inspires and teaches you to write your own stories. Thank you for reading this book, and good luck!

THIS IS THE LAST STRAW!" Hank yelled as he burst into Dr. Palindrome's office.

Hank was the janitor, and he was very angry. He was also very green. And not in the sense of being "full of envy" or "new to his job" or even "about to throw up." Hank was literally green. His skin was the exact same shade as the paint on the walls of Lab Six.

Lab Six was where, just moments before, Hank had mopped up an accidental spill. Dr. Salaam was experimenting with chameleon genes, and judging by the color of Hank's skin, the experiment had just taken an exciting new turn.

At least Dr. Salaam thought it was exciting. Hank did not agree.

"YOU PEOPLE ARE NUTS!" he screamed at Dr. Palindrome. "I QUIT!"

Dr. Palindrome sighed. He was the director of CEASE—the Center for Extremely Advanced Science Experiments. It was the world's most famous research lab, and the hardest part about running it was finding janitors. The average CEASE janitor worked for less than two weeks before either quitting, suffering a career-ending injury, or just mysteriously disappearing.

"Let's not be hasty, Hank," Dr. Palindrome said, pointing to one of the burgundy red leather chairs in his office. "Have a seat. We'll talk."

Hank sat down and glared at Dr. Palindrome.

"Now, why are you quitting?"

"Are you kidding? LOOK AT ME! I'M GREEN!"

"Actually, you're more of a burgundy red at the moment."

Hank looked down at his arms, which now blended in perfectly with the chair. "Oh, for crying out loud! That stuff turned me into a chameleon!"

Dr. Palindrome looked pained—not because of Hank, but because he was worried that whatever had turned Hank into a chameleon might have gotten on his chair. It was a very expensive chair, and Dr. Palindrome was quite fond of it.

"I'm terribly sorry, Hank. Although I'd like to point out that chameleonism WAS one of the occupational hazards listed in your employment contract. Still, it shouldn't be a problem as long as you spend the rest of your life standing next to things that are flesh-colored."

"If you had an ounce of shame, Doc, you'd shut this place down! It's irresponsible! It's life-threatening!"

Only for janitors, thought Dr. Palindrome. But he didn't say that out loud. Instead, he nodded sadly and said, "It's true there are risks. But you can't make an omelet without breaking some eggs. And of course, by 'omelet,' I mean 'amazing scientific discoveries.'"

And by "eggs," he thought to himself, *I mean "janitors."*

Dr. Palindrome had learned from experience that it was best to keep most of his thoughts about janitors to himself.

Hank understood what he meant anyway. "Go find

7

yourself another egg, you creep!" Hank yelled as he stormed out.

Dr. Palindrome scowled. He didn't like being called a creep. He didn't like finding janitors, either. But it was part of his job, so he picked up the phone to call the janitors' union and order another one.

Then he remembered. The janitors' union had banned CEASE from hiring any more of its members.

So had the temp agency, the job fair people, all the local schools, and the classified ad site that refused to run any more "janitor wanted" ads after some nasty business involving a radioactive gerbil.

This was a real problem. If they were forced to clean up their own highly dangerous spills, splicings, and subatomic particles, CEASE's scientists would start dropping like flies.

Without a janitor, CEASE might . . . cease.

Just the thought of it made Dr. Palindrome's forehead sweaty with fear.

Something had to be done, and quickly.

But what . . . ?

A chameleon janitor?! What kind of story is this? See page 202.

That same moment, a young man was standing outside CEASE's front door with a hopeful look on his face. His name was Tom Edison, and he was there to fulfill his dream of being a world-famous scientist.

Now, you may be thinking, "Wait a minute—isn't Tom Edison ALREADY a world-famous scientist?" Not exactly. Throughout history, there have been many Tom Edisons. And this was not THAT Tom Edison. He was simply A Tom Edison.

Since you'll be hearing a lot about this one, let's call him OUR Tom Edison.

Our Tom Edison loved everything about science. The life-changing discoveries! The exploring of the unknown! The mixing of occasionally dangerous chemicals! It was all very thrilling, and Tom dreamed of becoming not just a scientist, but an amazingly great one.

Unfortunately for Tom, he was terrible at science.

Even more unfortunately, he didn't realize it.

In school, his science grades had been awful. He got a D in Biology, an F in Chemistry, and an H in Physics (a grade that didn't even exist until Tom's teacher had to invent it to describe his performance). But bad grades didn't discourage Tom. He'd once heard that Albert Einstein—one of the greatest scientists in history—had flunked math as a kid.

This was a myth (Einstein's math grades were fantastic—after all, he was Einstein), but Tom didn't know that. So he decided his horrible grades were actually a sign that he was destined for Einstein-level greatness.

All he needed was a chance to prove himself.

He'd come to CEASE in search of that chance. This wasn't the first time. It wasn't even the tenth time. When your dream is to become a world-famous scientist, and there's a whole lab full of them just a bike ride away from your house, it's hard to resist dropping by, even if you never make it past the front desk.

Tom had never made it past the front desk. And if he'd been anyone else, he probably would've been banned from even coming near the place by now.

But he had one huge thing going for him: People really, really liked Tom. Everyone he met found him cheerful, kind, thoughtful, and fun to be around. CEASE's receptionist, Doris, was no exception.

Tom had brought Doris a jelly doughnut (her favorite), which was almost knocked out of his hand by the angry man who stormed out of CEASE just as Tom was walking in.

"Excuse me! Sorry! Have a great day!" Tom said with a smile. The man, whose face strangely resembled a red leather chair, stomped off without a word.

"Morning, Tom!" said Doris from behind the front desk.

"Hi, Doris! Would you like a doughnut? I got extra."

"That is SO nice of you!"

"My pleasure. Hey, want to hear my great idea for a new invention?"

"Fire away," said Doris through a mouthful of doughnut.

"An electroquantum box . . . powered by gamma radiokinesis . . . that can bring dead people back to life! Whaddaya think?"

"Did you get this idea from watching *Star Trip?*"

"Yes, I did!" Most of Tom's ideas for inventions came from *Star Trip.* He'd seen every episode at least three times. This was quite a feat, because when you included all of *Star Trip*'s companion series (like *Beyond Star Trip* and *Star Trip: Theta Quadrant*), there had been 927 episodes.

"You DO know all the science on that show is fake. Right, Tom?"

"Doris," Tom sighed, "we've discussed this. *Star Trip* takes place in the twenty-seventh century. So the electro-quantum box isn't fake, it just hasn't been invented yet! And I can be the one to invent it! All I need is a fluotanium capacitor ray!"

"Which is not a real thing—"

"Not yet! But if CEASE hires me, there could be a fluotanium capacitor ray in your future! Think about it, Doris."

"I will, Tom."

"So, can I get a job interview?"

"Not today. I'm sorry!" Doris wanted to help him. Really, she did. But according to Tom's resume (which he'd dropped off with her at least six times), his work experience as a scientist was limited to mixing dangerous chemicals in his garage. This didn't always go well. In fact, Tom's eyebrows were only just growing back after his latest experiment had ended very, very suddenly.

He DID have an advanced degree in chemistry, but it came from a place called "the University of Bobby Z." Doris had her doubts about the education Tom had gotten there.

But she had no doubt at all that if she passed one of Tom's resumes on to Dr. Palindrome, he'd fire her on the spot for wasting his time.

"Don't sweat it, Doris," Tom said cheerfully. "You'll come around eventually. How are Larry and the kids?"

"Doing great, thanks for asking! We're going to—oh, hello, Dr. Palindrome."

Dr. Palindrome had just come out of his office to ask Doris to call the local prison to find out if they had a work-release program for janitors. Tom gasped at the sight of one of his science heroes.

"Ohmygosh, Dr. Emo Palindrome! I am a HUGE fan, sir! I even own your Famous Scientist Trading Card!"

Dr. Palindrome was flattered . . . but also confused. "There are trading cards for famous scientists?"

"Sort of. I made them myself! So there's just the one set. But if you think about it, that makes them EXTREMELY RARE collector's items! And I am VERY honored to meet you, sir!" Tom stuck out his hand eagerly. Dr. Palindrome shook it with a wary look.

"And you are . . . ?"

"Tom Edison! Chemical reaction scientist!"

"And . . . what happened to your eyebrows?"

"Chemical reaction. Just, y'know— BOOM! And they were gone. But they're growing back fast! Sir, I am VERY interested in working for CEASE. Here's my resume!"

Doris winced as Tom handed Dr. Palindrome the spare resume he always kept in his back pocket. This probably wasn't going to end well for Tom.

Dr. Palindrome unfolded the resume and looked it over. "Edison . . . that sounds familiar . . . "

"You're probably thinking of the other Tom Edison? Inventor of the lightbulb? I'm not actually him—"

"I suspected that . . . since he's been dead for nearly a century."

"Right."

"Did you possibly"—Dr. Palindrome waggled Tom's resume—"leave this under the windshield of my car once?"

"More than once, yeah. That was me!"

"And it says here you got your PhD in chemistry from the . . . University of Bobby Z?"

"Yep! Good ol' UBZ!"

"Where's that located?"

"Mostly in the trunk of Bobby's car. He's got a real 'do-it-yourself' approach to education."

"I see. Well, Mr. Edison, why don't you and your unusual resume . . . "

Tom's eyes widened with hope. Doris's eyes squeezed shut with fear. Dr. Palindrome could be cruel at times, and she was sure this would be one of those times.

" . . . come into my office and have a chat?"

"Sure thing!"

By the time Doris opened her eyes in surprise, Dr. Palindrome was closing his office door behind Tom.

This Tom Edison guy seems important! Turn to page 205.

H ave a seat, Mr. Edison! Not in the red chair. Just to be safe."

Tom took a seat on the couch. He was too excited to wonder why it might not be safe to sit in the red chair. Dr. Palindrome took his usual spot behind his desk.

"So—" Dr. Palindrome began.

"Yes!"

"You're looking for a job?"

"Am I ever! Doc, if you give me a shot, I'll be the best scientist you've ever—"

"Here's the thing," Dr. Palindrome interrupted. "We're full up on scientists."

Tom's face fell. He was crushed.

"But . . . " Dr. Palindrome said.

Tom's face rose. A ray of hope!

"What would you say to being our janitor?"

Tom's face fell, then rose, then fell again. He was very confused. "Uh . . . would that be the kind of thing where I'd start as a janitor, then work my way up to scientist?"

"No. Sorry. It doesn't work that way."

"But could it? I mean, if I was really, really good?"

Dr. Palindrome shook his head. "Definitely not."

"Definitely definitely? Or just definitely?"

"Both. There's no chance."

Tom's face fell again. This time, it didn't get back up. "Gosh, I don't think . . . I mean, being a scientist is my dream! If I wound up here, just being a janitor? And that was all the other scientists saw me as? And there was no chance I'd ever be one of them? It'd break my heart. It really would."

Tom stood up. "But thanks. It was a real honor to meet you. It's just not the right fit—"

Dr. Palindrome could feel his forehead getting sweaty again. A perfectly good egg was about to walk right out the door. And there were no more chickens.

"I'm sorry," he said quickly. "Did I say 'no' chance? I meant 'a' chance."

"Really?" Tom's face was starting to hurt from all the rising and falling.

"Really!" Dr. Palindrome was smiling and nodding (and wiping sweat from his forehead).

"Really definitely?"

"Definitely really! Of course, you'd have to be a truly top-notch janitor. Willing to clean anything you're asked, no matter how dangerous or unstable—"

"ABSOLUTELY!" Tom yelled. "Ohmygosh! If it'd put me on track to become a scientist, I'd do ANYTHING for this job! I'd wrestle tigers!"

"What about genetically enhanced supermonkeys?" Dr. Palindrome asked. "Would you wrestle those?"

"I sure would!"

"Then welcome aboard!" said Dr. Palindrome, sticking his hand out with a smile.

Tom shook it happily. "FANTASTIC! When can I start?"

"How about now? That red chair could use a good scrubbing."

I've got a bad feeling about this Dr. P ... Find out why on page 211.

I n the darkest corner of the deepest basement at
CEASE—beyond the *screech* of Dr. Johnson's supermonkeys, the *bew* of Dr. Overtree's lasers, and the *yeeowch!* of
Dr. Lee, who kept forgetting to wear safety gloves when
handling strong acids—was a tiny, windowless lab. Inside,
surrounded by hundreds of beakers, burners, and sandwich wrappers, a single-minded young scientist was
working on the most important project of her life.

She'd been at it for years. She worked every day, for
hours and hours. She worked until her eyes got blurry
and her nose ran from the smell of the strange chemicals
cooking in her beakers. She worked until she fell asleep at
her lab table. Then she woke up and kept on working.

All the scientists at CEASE worked hard. But nobody
worked harder than Dr. Marisa Morice.

The other scientists didn't know this. Because Marisa was the first to arrive and the last to leave, and because she rarely stepped out of her little lab except to get take-out sandwiches from the cafeteria, most of them had no idea she was there.

In fact, they didn't even know she existed.

If this bothered Marisa (and it did, a lot), she told herself it would all change once she'd made her big break-through. When the others found out what she'd been working on all these years, they'd be so amazed that she'd instantly become the most famous and popular scientist of them all!

Or at least popular enough that some of them would want to eat lunch with her.

Or even just one of them.

Sometimes, she daydreamed about becoming friends with Dr. Vasquez. They had a lot in common: They were both young, female, and excited about science. On top of that, Dr. Vasquez had qualities Marisa desperately wished she had, too: confidence, friendliness, and outstanding fingernails. They were always brightly painted and perfectly trimmed in a way that was stylish, but not too long to get in the way of serious lab work.

Marisa's own fingernails were bitten to the quick.

Whenever she got stuck on a thorny science problem, she chewed them ragged, so caught up in her thoughts that she hardly realized she was doing it. There must be a secret trick to remembering not to chew your fingernails. In Marisa's daydreams, Dr. Vasquez would tell her all about it as they bonded over lunch.

But at the moment, Dr. Vasquez didn't know she existed. And Marisa was far too shy to introduce herself. So until she finished her big invention and announced it to the world, she was all alone—tucked away in her tiny, windowless lab, chewing her fingernails to bits, and eating her lonely little sandwiches . . .

Then the new janitor showed up.

"OHMYGOSH! Aren't you Marisa Morice? The youngest winner in the history of the National Junior Science Competition? HOLY COW! You were Rookie of the Year in my Famous Scientist Trading Card set!"

"Who are you, and why don't you have any eyebrows?" Marisa's voice quivered. Her heart was pounding like a jackhammer. CEASE's janitors never lasted long enough to empty her wastebasket, so it had been a long time since another person had set foot in her lab. Let alone someone with no eyebrows.

"Long story. They're growing back, though! And sorry! I didn't mean to scare you. I'm the new janitor. Tom Edison! But not THAT Tom Edison. I'm a huge fan! When you won that science contest? And you were just twelve years old? I was twelve, too! I saw you on TV, and it was so inspiring! You're what made ME want to become a scientist!"

Marisa blushed. She was very flattered. Winning the National Junior Science Competition had been the high point of her life, and no one had mentioned it in years.

But she was also very confused. "Aren't you a . . . janitor?"

"Yeah. It's temporary, though. I'm working my way up!"

"I don't think that's how it—"

"Oh, wow, MARISA MORICE! This is so exciting! So what happened after you won that contest? Whatcha been up to these past . . . oh, geez, ten years?"

"I've been . . . down here." Marisa's spirits, which had briefly soared at the mention of her past triumph, quickly crashed again. She didn't like being reminded that after that fleeting, heady moment of fame, she'd spent the next ten years alone and ignored.

"The whole time? Wow! You must be up to something AMAZING!" Tom looked around. "Are you inventing a new kind of sandwich wrapper?"

22

"Huh? Oh. No. I just . . . eat in a lot."

"Want me to clean these up for you?"

"I can do it my—"

"SUPER!" Tom began cleaning up the wrappers as fast as he could. "Hey, if you ever need help with your research? Let me know!"

"I don't think you'd—"

"I'm a scientist, too! I have a PhD in chemistry!"

"Really?" As unlikely as a PhD-holding janitor seemed, Marisa perked up at the thought of a possible lab partner. "Could you affix a graphene PSC to a polyethylene naphthalate substrate?"

Tom looked frightened. There were at least five words in that sentence he'd never heard before.

"Oh, wow. Geez. Umm . . . let me just get the sandwich wrappers."

"Okay."

"Yeah!" He gathered the last of the wrappers. "Anything else I can do?"

"Um . . . no?"

"Great! Hey, if you ever need anything—want me to bring you a sandwich or something—just give a yell!"

"Okay. I probably won't."

"That's fine, too! Bye!"

The new janitor shut the door, leaving Marisa alone again. She let out a shaky sigh. Talking to people was stressful. She wasn't very good at it. How long had it been since she'd even had lunch with someone?

Wait a minute . . . .

Had that janitor just asked if she wanted him to bring her a sandwich?

That was almost like asking someone to have lunch!

Should she have said yes? Had she just missed her first chance in years to eat lunch with someone?

No. There would be other chances. Once the world found out about her big breakthrough, everyone would want to have lunch with her.

And she'd never be lonely again.

She put her head down and went back to work.

Can a story have TWO main characters? Turn to page 214.

Tom's first two weeks as CEASE's janitor were a huge success. He cleaned up fourteen toxic spills, put out six laser fires, captured two escaped supermonkeys, and even managed to get rid of the small black hole in Dr. Palavi's office that had swallowed three previous janitors.

And he'd done it all for the price of just two second-degree burns, one mysterious blue rash, half a missing finger, and a monkey bite that he'd secretly hoped

Supermonkeys, mini black holes, AND a cafeteria? This is some setting for a story! Learn more on page 217.

would give him superpowers (but, sadly, all it had given him was a bacterial infection).

By CEASE janitor standards, this was an amazing record.

Even more amazing, Tom quickly became the most popular person in the CEASE cafeteria. Every day at lunch, a dozen scientists crowded around his table to eat nachos (Tom's favorite food) and play a game he'd made up called Stump the Janitor.

The object was to come up with a trivia question about *Star Trip* that Tom couldn't answer. It was almost impossible to win—in the two weeks they'd been playing, only Dr. Vasquez had ever stumped Tom, with "What's the only way to kill a Gorgstomper?" But her victory was overturned when a search of the *Star Trip Encyclopedia* proved that no one had ever managed to kill a Gorgstomper at all.

Dr. Vasquez didn't mind. She loved playing Stump the Janitor. So did the other scientists. There was a whole table full of them, laughing and chatting with Tom, on the day Marisa skipped into the cafeteria in the middle of the lunch hour to get a take-out sandwich.

Marisa didn't usually skip, but this day was special.

Skipping to the sandwich station, she ordered turkey on rye with bacon and avocado.

Most days, she didn't get the bacon and avocado, because they cost extra.

But again, this day was special.

It was so special that Marisa was smiling from ear to ear as she waited for her sandwich. Then her eye fell on the table full of happily chattering scientists.

They certainly looked like they were having a good time over there. It was like a giant lunch party. And who was that in the middle of it?

Was that the new janitor?

How could that be? He was new. And a janitor! How could he be so popular?

And was he staring right at her?

Awkward! Embarrassing! She gasped and turned away. Fortunately, her sandwich was ready.

From across the cafeteria, Tom saw Dr. Morice at the sandwich station. She seemed to be alone, so he decided to invite her to sit with them.

"Back in a flash!" he told Dr. Salaam, who was about to take her turn at Stump the Janitor.

The scientists all smiled as they watched him trot across the room.

"That Tom is fun in a bucket," said Dr. Pulaski.

"He really is," said Dr. Lee. "You know, sometimes I spill things on purpose just so he'll hang out in my lab while he cleans it up!"

"No kidding? I thought I was the only one who did that!"

"I sure hope he lasts longer than the other janitors," said Dr. Salaam.

The laughter and chatter suddenly stopped. The scientists all looked at each other nervously.

Finally, Dr. Overtree broke the silence. "He'll be fine! A guy like that always lands on his feet!"

"Tell me about it," said Dr. Palavi. "Remember that mini black hole in my office that kept eating janitors? Tom got rid of it for me! Without a scratch! Well, he DID lose half a finger. But that's not bad."

The mood around the table brightened. Half a janitor's finger seemed like a pretty good trade-off for getting rid of a black hole.

"You can't make an omelet without breaking some eggs," Dr. Lee said. All the other scientists nodded in agreement.

Then Dr. Pulaski coughed awkwardly. "As long as we're talking about the guy behind his back . . . is everybody okay with not telling Tom there's no chance a janitor can ever become a scientist?"

"Of course!" Dr. Overtree bellowed. "What do you want us to do, break his heart?"

Everyone nodded again. The truth would be painful, and nobody wanted to see Tom unhappy.

Meanwhile, Tom had reached the sandwich station a moment too late to catch Marisa, who was headed for the door at high speed.

"Hey, Dr. Morice!" he yelled after her. "Want to have lunch with us?"

It was too late. She was gone. Disappointed, he went back to the others.

"Who was that woman you were yelling at?" Dr. Salaam asked.

"Dr. Morice."

"Who?"

Tom couldn't believe it. "Marisa Morice? Child genius? The world's youngest-ever winner of the National Junior Science Competition?"

"Not ringing a bell," said Dr. Lee.

"Is she new here?" asked Dr. Vasquez.

Back in her tiny basement lab, it took several minutes for Marisa's heart to stop racing. She couldn't be sure, but she thought the new janitor might have yelled something at her as she was rushing out of the cafeteria.

He might even have been inviting her to lunch.

Had she missed her chance to make friends? Again?

Or was he just playing a joke on her? What if they all were? What if all the other scientists were up in the cafeteria right now, laughing at her?

In the end, she decided it didn't matter. Because today was special.

It was the day she finally had her big breakthrough. The secret project she'd been slaving away at for years was complete.

When the other scientists saw what she'd come up with, they'd be amazed. They'd be in awe! They'd fall all over themselves asking to have lunch with her!

She smiled through a mouthful of turkey on rye with bacon and avocado.

It was time to schedule a Show and Tell.

Show and Tells were the most exciting thing about working at CEASE. When a scientist's latest discovery was ready to share with others, they held a Show and Tell for everyone at the center. What began at a CEASE Show and Tell often ended in a Nobel Prize, a world-changing new product, a billion-dollar company, or all of the above.

When she walked into the director's office, Marisa was so excited she could hardly breathe.

"Dr. Palindrome?"

"Hello! Dr. . . . Murray, isn't it?"

"Morice, actually."

"Right! Michelle Morice!"

"Marisa Morice."

"Sorry! It takes me a little while to learn names."

"I've been here for ten years."

"And we're SO glad to have you! What can I help you with, Marina?"

Marisa didn't bother to correct him again. He'd remember her name soon enough. "I'd like to schedule a Show and Tell?"

"Wonderful! How soon?"

"As soon as possible?"

Dr. Palindrome checked his calendar. "How about tomorrow?"

"Okay. Great!"

"Super! Dr. Vasquez is also doing a Show and Tell. So we'll combine the two. A double feature!"

Marisa's heart leaped. Maybe tomorrow would be the day she and Dr. Vasquez finally had lunch! "Sure thing!"

Then she thought about it some more, and her excitement turned to worry. Marisa had no idea what Dr. Vasquez had planned. What if it upstaged Marisa's big invention?

No. How could that be? Marisa had worked on hers for ten years! It had to be at least as good as whatever Dr. Vasquez had planned. There was no reason to worry.

But Marisa worried anyway.

☾ ☾ ☾

The next afternoon, fifty-eight scientists and a janitor

gathered in CEASE's auditorium for its first-ever double Show and Tell.

Marisa and Dr. Vasquez stood on the stage with Dr. Palindrome. Marisa stood next to a small table, covered in a black sheet. Dr. Vasquez, her fingernails painted the perfect shade of red for the occasion, stood next to a wheeled cart topped by a mysterious giant box the size of a double-wide refrigerator. It was covered in a much larger (and, Marisa had to admit, much nicer) black sheet than Marisa's.

"So!" Dr. Palindrome's voice boomed. "What will you two be showing us today?"

"You first," said Dr. Vasquez to Marisa with a friendly smile.

"Ummm . . . okay."

Marisa stepped forward, her whole body trembling. It was only her confidence in the invention she was announcing that kept her from either fainting or running from the room.

Her voice barely rose above a whisper. Even through the microphone, the other scientists had to strain to hear her.

"I've . . . um . . . built a working solar-cell prototype—" Marisa felt herself getting dizzy and had to pause for a moment to breathe—"that combines graphene and molybdenum disulfide to a thickness of twenty thousand nanometers."

Marisa pulled the black sheet off the table to reveal a solar panel the size and shape of a small windowpane.

A murmur of surprise went through the crowd. There was even a gasp or two.

"That's AMAZING!" yelled Tom. "What does it mean?"

"It's, um, ten times more efficient than current panels," Marisa answered. "So, um, it's, uh, kind of a revolution in solar energy. That, um, will solve mankind's energy needs forever with, um, zero harm to the environment."

"OHMYGOSH!" yelled Tom. "That is DEFINITELY AMAZING!" He looked around. "Right?"

Tom was right. The other scientists were all nodding, smiling, and whispering to each other with excitement.

As she watched them from the stage, Marisa's nervousness melted away. Her face could barely contain her smile.

Just look at them! They were so excited! They loved her invention! Even Dr. Vasquez was beaming, and she'd just been upstaged!

This was the moment Marisa had been waiting ten years to enjoy.

It felt even better than she'd dreamed. The scientists were all waving their hands in the air, desperate to quiz her about the solar panels. Or possibly to invite her to lunch! She wasn't sure which. But she couldn't wait to find out.

Dr. Palindrome cleared his throat, quieting the crowd. "Now, I'm sure you all have a lot of questions for Dr. Moran—"

"Morice," Marisa corrected him, with a confidence that surprised even her. "Sorry."

"Not at all! Morice! Right! My apologies. But before we get to the questions, let's not forget Dr. Vasquez. Have you got something for us that's even more amazing than a solution to all of mankind's energy needs?"

"I think I do," said Dr. Vasquez. "I've invented a time machine."

She whipped the sheet off her giant box, revealing a six-foot-tall, five-foot-wide contraption made of metal and glass.

The room exploded with noise as fifty-seven scientists and a janitor went completely bonkers.

"WHAAAAAAAT?"

"OHMYGOSH!"

"I CAN'T BELIEVE IT!"

Marisa couldn't believe it, either. "Seriously? But . . . isn't time travel impossible?"

"Not anymore!" said Dr. Vasquez in a perky voice. "Who wants to see how it works?"

Fifty-eight hands shot in the air.

"WE DO!"

"SHOW US!"

"OH WOW OH WOW!"

Dr. Vasquez opened a human-sized door on the side of the time machine. Inside, there was just enough room for two people to stand.

"There are controls inside that the user can set to any date and time in Earth's history. But because of the risk involved in sending a human on its first test run, I've built a remote control to operate the machine from outside."

She pointed to a bright orange box hanging from a pair of hooks on the side of the time machine.

"I call this gizmo a 'fetcher,' because it'll fetch the machine to and from any date I request. Would you like to see a demonstration?"

"WOULD WE EVER!"

"HECK, YEAH!"

"ZOWEEE!"

Everyone was on their feet, yelling with excitement.

Everyone, that is, except Marisa. She stood off to one side of the stage, looking pale and slightly barfy. The moment of her dreams suddenly felt a lot less dreamy. In fact, it was starting to feel more like a nightmare.

Dr. Vasquez unhooked the bread box–sized fetcher from the side of the machine. "I've programmed the fetcher to send the machine back in time to 10,000 B.C. for exactly five minutes, then return to this very spot ten seconds from now.

She placed her finger on a big red button on the fetcher's display panel.

Everyone in the room sucked in their breath with excitement. (Except for Marisa. She was clutching her stomach and trying not to be sick.)

Dr. Vasquez paused. "Before we start," she warned, "there's a slight chance this will go horribly wrong and create a small but extremely dangerous black hole. In which case . . . "

She turned her eyes to Tom and gave him a hopeful look.

Tom raised his hand and yelled, "I can clean that up for you! I've got nine-and-a-half fingers left!"

"Thanks, Tom! You're the best!" Dr. Vasquez gave him a thumbs-up. "So, goodbye, time machine. We'll see you again in ten seconds!"

Dr. Vasquez pressed the button on the fetcher.

The time machine disappeared. Only the wheeled cart remained, spinning in place on the stage.

Everyone in the room gasped in wonder . . . except Marisa, who was very dizzy and had just lurched offstage in search of somewhere to sit before she fainted.

Dr. Vasquez watched the fetcher's display panel as she counted down:

"Four . . . three . . . two . . . one—"

That time machine really spoiled Marisa's plan! See page 221.

POP! With a noise like a cork getting pulled from a bottle, the time machine reappeared on its wheeled cart.

But it looked very different. The gleaming new box was no longer gleaming or new-looking. Its roof and three sides were pockmarked with fist-sized dents. The fourth side looked like it had been dunked in a vat of mud. And on the side opposite the mud, an enormous dent had bowed in the machine's entire lower half. It looked like some giant horned animal had rammed it at high speed.

"Oh, my!" declared Dr. Vasquez with a grin. "It looks like 10,000 B.C. was a pretty rough place."

The scientists began gasping, cheering, and yelling all at once. They were shocked! They were amazed! They had questions.

The only person in the room who wasn't talking—or even listening—was Marisa. As the other scientists all crowded around Dr. Vasquez and her muddy, dented, mind-blowing invention, Marisa sat in a corner with her head between her knees.

The moment of triumph she'd been working toward for ten years had lasted all of ten seconds. And now everyone was falling all over some other scientist, leaving Marisa as forgotten and ignored as before.

It wasn't fair. It wasn't right.

Maybe if she just closed her eyes for a little while, it'd all go away.

She tried that. It didn't work. When she opened her eyes again, the whole crowd was heading out the door, chattering with excitement, practically carrying Dr. Vasquez on their shoulders.

Dr. Palindrome was saying something about a party. The new janitor was yelling, "Nachos for everybody!"

As usual, nobody thought to invite Marisa.

Then they were gone. She was left alone with a time machine, a solar panel, and a terrible ache in her stomach.

Or maybe it was her heart. It was hard to tell. Everything in there ached.

Marisa stared at the machine on the stage. Could it really be true? Could this big, muddy refrigerator be an actual TIME MACHINE?

Either Dr. Vasquez had just come up with the most amazing invention in the history of the world . . . or it was all a hoax.

Ohmygosh!

What if it's a hoax?

A scam?

A magic trick?

After all, what proof did anyone have that this machine had just gone back to 10,000 B.C.? Some mud?

There was plenty of mud just behind the building. A bunch of dents? No reason those couldn't be made in the present.

It had to be a hoax. Sure, Dr. Vasquez seemed friendly and trustworthy, with a warm smile and perfect fingernails. But didn't all con artists seem that way? What was more likely—that she'd solved one of the greatest challenges in the history of the universe or that she'd tricked everybody with a fake time machine?

Marisa's heart began to beat faster. This was a disaster in the making. What would happen when Dr. Vasquez announced her so-called time machine to the world and the truth came out? CEASE would be ruined! The whole center would become the laughingstock of the world! Its reputation would never recover!

Unless Marisa saved them all.

If she could prove the time machine was a hoax before the rest of the world found out about it, Dr. Vasquez would be ruined. But Marisa would have rescued everyone at CEASE from being ruined along with her.

Then they'd remember that Dr. Vasquez wasn't the only one who'd come up with an amazing invention that day.

The ache Marisa was feeling began to go away. She had a job to do.

She got up and approached the time machine.

◑ ◒ ◓

The front door of CEASE burst open. Fifty-seven scientists, a janitor, and a receptionist (they'd picked up Doris along the way) emerged, heading for the restaurant across the street. The moment was too big and exciting for a simple cafeteria celebration, so Dr. Palindrome had called the restaurant to reserve a table for fifty-nine and place a very large order of nachos.

Suddenly, Dr. Vasquez stopped. The others stopped with her.

She turned to Tom. "I hate to mention this, buddy, but if that mud dries, it's going to be a real bear to clean up."

Right away, Tom saw what she was getting at. "I'm your man, doc! I'll wash that mud off, pronto!" He turned to head back into CEASE.

"Wait!"

"Yeah, Doc?"

"Unhook the fetcher first. If it gets wet, it could leak deadly radioactive goo. I don't want you to get hurt."

"Good to know. Thanks for the tip!"

"And whatever you do, don't open the door of the machine. And if you DO open the door, DON'T pull the green lever."

"Unhook the fetcher, don't get it wet, no door, no green lever. Got it!"

"You're the best, Tom!" Dr. Vasquez yelled as he ran off.

"Save me some nachos!" he yelled back happily.

When Tom came back into the auditorium, the time machine's door was open.

He gasped and ran to the machine. Inside it, he found Marisa. She was standing in front of the control panel, staring at its large green lever.

Tom gasped again.

The gasp startled her. She jumped—and when she did, her arm struck the green lever, nudging it forward.

"AAAAAAAH!" Tom screamed.

The scream startled Marisa even more. She jumped again—and her arm knocked the green lever even farther forward.

"NYAHHH!" Tom screamed again.

This time, Marisa wasn't startled. She was annoyed.

"Will you stop screaming?"

"You're going to start the time machine!"

"It's not a time machine. It's a hoax!"

Tom looked at her, confused. "Uh . . . no, I'm pretty sure it's a time machine."

Marisa sighed. "What's more likely—that Dr. Vasquez figured out how to rip a hole in the fabric of space-time? Or that she faked it, and time travel is impossible?"

"Time travel IS possible!" Tom insisted. "It happens all the time on *Star Trip*."

"Oh, for crying out loud," said Dr. Morice. "*Star Trip* is fake! Just like this!"

She waved her arms in the air . . . and knocked the green lever still further forward.

"YAAAAAAH!"

"Will you please stop screaming?"

"Just don't touch that green lever again!" Tom pleaded with her.

"What, THIS green lever?" she asked, and pushed it all the way forward.

The lever disappeared.

So did the time machine.

And because they were standing in it, so did Tom and Marisa.

I t's impossible to describe the feeling of traveling through space-time at one thousand years per second.

But Tom tried anyway.

"This feels suuuuuuper-weird," he said.

And he was right. The feeling of having your body flattened into a sheet one atom thick, twisted around itself half a million times, and then put back together exactly as it was before is nothing if not suuuuuuper-weird.

Marisa would have agreed with Tom if she'd heard him. But her ears had just been flattened into a sheet one atom thick, so she didn't quite catch what he'd said.

And then . . .

Just like that . . .

POP!

They were standing in the machine, exactly as they had been a few seconds ago. Marisa looked past Tom, out the open door behind him, and gasped.

Tom turned to see what Marisa was looking at. "Oh, geez! We left the door open!"

Half a second later, he realized that not only was the door open, but it no longer led into the CEASE auditorium. Outside the doorway was a narrow, rocky shelf, with a steep hillside looming above on the right and a sharp cliff on the left.

"OHMYGOSH! WHERE ARE WE?"

Marisa quickly glanced out of the time machine's three small windows, each looking out a different side. "Looks like we're perched on a ledge . . . at the edge of a cliff . . . high above a lake . . . with a huge hill right behind us."

"WHEN ARE WE?"

Marisa looked at the control panel next to the green lever. "10,000 B.C.?"

"HOLY JAMOLEY!"

"Will you please stop yelling?"

"Sorry! I've just never traveled through time before."

"Well, you're about to do it again," said Marisa, pulling the green lever back toward her.

This time, the lever didn't disappear.

47

Neither did anything else.

Marisa pushed it forward.

Nothing happened.

She pulled it back again.

Still nothing.

Forward.Back.Forward.Back—

"Don't break it!" yelled Tom.

"I'm not! I'm just trying to go home!" Marisa could feel her heart pound against her ribs. Her breath was coming in shallow, rapid bursts.

Tom thought for a second. "Wait—I think we have to use the fetcher! It's hanging on the hooks outside the machine!"

"Can you go get it?" asked Marisa. She wasn't too hot on the idea of stepping outside herself.

"Sure thing," Tom said, and stepped out the door.

He found himself on a narrow, rocky ledge a hundred feet above the shore of a small lake. Above the ledge, a steep hill rose another fifty feet behind them to a boulder-strewn ridge.

The sun was shining. Birds were chirping. 10,000 B.C. actually seemed quite nice.

Except for the fact that the time machine was teetering on the edge of a cliff.

And the fetcher was hanging
from the side that stuck out
over the edge.

YIKES!
They're in the
Stone Age! NOW they've
got a problem!
See page 227.

"Oh, geez," Tom said.

"What is it?" Marisa called to him
from inside the machine.

"That fetcher's gonna be tough
to reach without plummeting to my
death. Heeeey, wait a minute . . ."

The time machine Tom had walked
into was muddy on one side, nearly caved in on the other,
and pockmarked with small dents. But the one he'd
stepped out of was as gleaming new as when Dr. Vasquez
first unveiled it.

"This time machine's good as new!" Tom told Marisa.
"Come out and look at this!"

"I'd rather not," she said.

"How come?"

"What if it leaves without us?"

"So why am I out here?"

"That's up to you."

Tom quickly stepped back inside. "Okay, here's the
thing. The machine looks brand-new. No mud, no dents,
no huge caved-in side, nothing. What's up with that?"

They both thought for a moment. Then Tom had an idea.

"Did you ever see that *Star Trip* episode where the *Formidable* went back in time, and Lieutenant Modi got eaten by a Chocksnark, so Captain Dirk sent them back a second time, only that time he tricked the Chocksnark into eating a Gundulzort instead?"

"I don't watch *Star Trip.*"

"How can you not watch *Star Trip?* It's the greatest show ever!"

"I just don't. It seems kind of silly."

"AAAAGH! How can you say that? What kind of scientist doesn't like *Star Trip?*"

"Did you have a point to make?"

"Only that *Star Trip* is the greatest show in the history of—"

"Not about *Star Trip!* About the fact that we're stuck in the Stone Age!"

"Oh! Right . . . Yes! Sorry. I'm thinking the fetcher was still programmed for Dr. Vasquez's demonstration? So it sent us back to the exact same place and time. And we're just repeating what happened all over again."

Marisa thought about this for a moment. "So all we

have to do," she said, "is sit in this machine for five minutes, and it'll send us right back to the present."

"Exactly!"

"That's great. Except for one thing."

"What?"

PLUNK! Something hard and loud struck the side of the machine.

"Shut the door!" Marisa yelled at Tom. He reached back and closed it just as—

PLUNK!

PLUNK!

PLUNK-PLUNK-PLUNK!

It was like sitting inside a car during a hailstorm.

Except it wasn't hail. It was something much more dangerous.

"Where are all those rocks coming from?"

"THOSE guys." Marisa was peering out the machine's back window, her head tilted so she could see up the steep hill that rose behind them. "Take a look."

She stepped back to give Tom room to look out the window himself.

"OHMYGOSH! ACTUAL CAVEMEN!" There were three of them atop the ridge—short, thin, bearded, and shaggy-haired men wearing what looked like animal-skin gym shorts.

"You shouldn't call them that," Marisa said. "I doubt they actually live in caves."

At the moment, where the men lived was much less important than what they were doing: hurling rocks down the hillside at the time machine.

PLUNK!

PLUNK!

PLUNK!

"This is so amazing!" yelled Tom. "Cavemen are trying to kill us! It's just like that episode of *Star Trip* when they went to the parallel universe where civilization never developed!"

"Could you not yell everything at the top of your lungs?"

"I'm sorry. It's just really exciting."

"It's not exciting," said Marisa. "It's terrifying." She tried to take a deep breath to calm herself down, but it didn't work.

PLUNK!

PLUNK!

PLUNK-PLUNK-PLUNK-PLUNK!

"Why's it so terrifying? We know what happens! The time machine goes back to the present!"

"With one side covered in mud—and the other side caved in. How do you think THAT happens?"

"Oh, geez." Tom looked out the window again. The cavemen had stopped throwing rocks. Instead, they were now rolling a large boulder sideways along the top of the ridge.

"They're going to roll that giant boulder down the hill and knock us off the cliff, aren't they?" Tom asked.

"Yes, they are."

"You think we'll be okay?"

"Definitely not."

"We'll survive, though, right?"

"Not a chance."

"Not even if we brace ourselves?"

"Did you take physics?"

"Yeah. But I got an H in it."

"What's an H?"

"It's a little worse than a G."

"What's a—?" Marisa stopped herself. There was no time. "Look, we're in a metal box. No seat belts. No air bags. Nothing to hold on to. And we're about to get hit by a . . . "—she looked out the window and did some quick math in her head—"call it a two-thousand-pound boulder accelerating down a fifty-foot hill at a forty-degree grade. Then we'll free-fall another hundred feet before we hit the mud on the edge of the lake. The odds of our surviving that are worse than your physics grade."

"OHMYGOSH, THEY'RE AN I?!" Tom yelled. "What are we going to do?"

"Jump out, climb down the cliff, and get back inside before the time machine leaves."

"I don't think that's a good idea."

"Neither is dying." She looked out the window. The cavemen had rolled the boulder into place directly above them and were starting to push it down the steep hill.

"Are you sure about this?" Tom asked.

Instead of answering, Marisa pushed past him, opened the door, and jumped out.

Tom took a deep breath and followed her.

CRASH!!

The boulder struck the time machine just as Tom jumped clear of it. He landed on the rocky ledge next to Marisa. As he began to get up, there was another—

CRASH!!

The second crash came from somewhere far below him. He peeked over the edge of the cliff. A hundred feet down, sunk into the muck on the shore of the lake, was the crumpled time machine.

"Oh, wow," said Tom. "That DEFINITELY would've killed us."

Marisa didn't answer. She was too busy sprinting away across the ledge.

"Where are you going?" Tom yelled.

Then he remembered. They had to get to the time

machine before the five minutes were up.

How many minutes had passed already? Two? Two-and-a-half? Thr—

"OWW!" Something sharp and heavy hit Tom in the upper arm. He looked up.

The three cavemen were staring down at him from the hilltop above.

They looked very angry.

And they were all holding rocks.

They cocked their arms back to throw.

Tom sprinted after Marisa as a volley of rocks clattered behind him.

PLUNK!

CLUNK!

PLUNK-CLUNK!

Up ahead, the ledge took a sharp turn. Marisa rounded the corner. When she saw what was up ahead, she stopped short.

The ledge went on for a hundred yards—and then disappeared, melting into the sheer rock wall of the cliff. There was no way to get from the ledge down to the time machine.

And the clock was ticking away. There was no time to go back and try running in the other direction.

If she wanted to make it to the time machine before it disappeared, she'd have to jump.

Which would probably kill her.

Unless . . .

Directly below, where the cliff and the ledge both turned sharply, there was no muddy shore. Instead, the lake's waters lapped against the cliff wall itself.

As Marisa peered down at the natural swimming hole, Tom came barreling around the corner, nearly knocking her off the ledge.

"Watch out!"

"Sorry!"

She pointed down to the water below. "How deep do you think that is?"

"I dunno. A few feet?"

"More than six?"

"No idea. Why?"

"If it's less than six, this is really going to hurt."

"What is?"

Instead of answering, Marisa jumped off the cliff. Tom gasped.

An endless second later, she hit the water and disappeared.

"DR. MORICE?" Tom yelled.

Marisa's head bobbed up from below the surface, so far away it looked to Tom like it was the size of a pea.

"ARE YOU OKAY?" he yelled.

"POINT YOUR TOES WHEN YOU HIT THE WATER!" she yelled back.

"WHY?" he yelled again.

"BECAUSE OF PHYSICS!" she yelled. Then she started to swim around the turn in the cliff, headed for the time machine.

"DO I HAVE TO JUMP?" he yelled. "I'M NOT GOOD AT PHYSICS!" He was also—to be completely honest—not good at swimming.

Actually, that was an understatement. Technically, speaking, Tom couldn't swim at all.

Maybe he should just—

"OWWW!" A rock hit him in the upper back. He looked up. The cavemen were letting fly with another round.

Tom jumped off the cliff.

It

felt

like

it

took

forever

to

hit

the

SPLASH!!!

A moment later, his head broke the surface, sputtering and gasping. He could see Dr. Morice fifty feet away, making the turn around the point toward the spot where the time machine had landed.

He dog-paddled after her as best he could and managed to thrash his way to the rock outcropping of the point. When he got that far, gasping for breath, he could see Marisa ahead of him. She was halfway to the shore where the time machine lay.

Tom kept going, but his legs were getting tired and starting to sink. As he reached the shallower water, his left foot brushed the lake bed and caught on something, yanking him back sharply.

Tom windmilled his arms and kicked as hard as he could, but he couldn't free his foot. The harder he tried, the more stuck he seemed to get.

Suddenly, it was very hard to keep his head above water.

And this made it very hard to breathe.

◑ ◔ ◐

Marisa had just reached dry land and started running, less than a hundred feet from the time machine, when she heard the half-gurgled scream.

"HEE-GL-EELP!"

She looked back. Tom was thrashing in the deep water, his head half-submerged.

Was he drowning?

Did he need her help?

He'd be fine. It wasn't serious. He yelled about everything. He was a yeller.

She kept running.

"HEEE-GLGLGLG!"

This time, the gurgling cut off Tom's yell entirely.

Marisa stopped.

In a split second, she tried to guess how much time she had left before the time machine vanished. She knew it wasn't much. And swimming back out to rescue Tom would take up most of it.

She had to make a choice.

Marisa turned around, plunged back into the water, and swam to Tom.

"HEGLGLGLPHT!"

"Hold still!"

Tom held still.

Marisa dove under the water.

His foot was caught in the fork of a submerged tree root.

She pried the sides of the root apart. Tom's foot slipped free.

When she surfaced, he tried to thank her, but his mouth was full of water.

And she was already twenty feet away, swimming for shore.

She reached land.

She sprinted to the machine.

The door had slammed itself shut. She reached down to open it.

But it was stuck in the muck. The door wouldn't open.

She pulled harder.

It still wouldn't open.

She kept pulling.

Tom arrived. He pulled, too.

They both pulled together and . . .

SPLUCK! The door came unstuck, flying open with such force that they both fell backward into the mud.

When they did, the door slammed shut again.

Marisa leaped up, yanked open the door again, and—POP!

The time machine disappeared.

Marisa didn't.

Neither did Tom.

They looked at each other, spattered in mud . . . on the shore of a lake . . . at the base of a cliff . . . stranded in the year 10,000 B.C.

Hoo-boy! Now we're REALLY stuck in the Stone Age! See page 231.

Tom stared at the six-inch-deep rectangle in the mud where the time machine had been.

"Oh, geez," he said.

Marisa's heart was thumping like a jackrabbit. Her breath was coming in rapid-fire huffs. She was on the brink of a full-blown panic attack.

"Hoo-boy," said Tom, slowly shaking his head.

Something deep inside Marisa's brain suddenly shifted gears, and her panic made a sharp detour into rage.

"This is some tough biscuits," Tom declared.

Marisa kicked him hard in the seat of his pants.

"YOWWW! What'd you kick me for?"

"ARE YOU KIDDING ME?! You ruined our lives, and all you can say is 'TOUGH BISCUITS?!'" Marisa's voice was getting hoarse. She'd done more yelling in the past five minutes than in all of the past five years.

"I didn't ruin our lives! You're the one who pulled the lever!"

It was a fair point. But Marisa kicked him again anyway.

"OWW! Cut it out!"

"Why can't you swim?!"

"I didn't know it was part of my job!"

They might have kept fighting for hours. But just then, the three cavemen appeared, swimming around the point. They'd followed her and Tom off the cliff. And they were surprisingly strong swimmers, especially considering that they were all carrying rocks.

"They're coming after us!" Marisa started scanning the shore for rocks of her own to use as weapons.

"There's only one thing we can do," Tom said. "We'll just have to—"

"Kill them," Marisa said.

"—make friends with them," Tom finished. "Wait—what?!"

"Find some rocks! Quick! While they're still in deep water!" There was an unfortunate shortage of deadly sized rocks on the shore. Plenty of giant boulders and tiny pebbles were lying around, but not much in between.

"We don't have to get violent!" Tom pleaded with Marisa.

"Yes, we do! They're trying to kill us!" Finally, Marisa found a decent-sized rock and hurled it at the cavemen. It missed the closest one's head by inches. He bellowed in anger and swam even faster toward them.

Marisa started searching for more rocks. But Tom wasn't ready to give up on diplomacy.

"WE COME IN PEACE!" he called out to the cavemen.

If she weren't so busy trying to save their lives, Marisa would have kicked him again. "THEY DON'T SPEAK ENGLISH! Grab some rocks!"

Tom thought for a moment. Then he tried again.

"HOLA, AMIGOS! MI NOMBRE ES—"

"THEY DON'T SPEAK SPANISH, EITHER!"

Secretly, Tom was relieved. His Spanish was terrible.

But now he was all out of languages. The cavemen were closing in. If he didn't think of something quick, there was going to be a rock fight to the death.

Tom was pretty sure he and Marisa would lose.

Suddenly, he had an idea. Like all of his ideas, it came from a *Star Trip* episode. He reached into the pocket of his pants—still soaking wet from the swim—and pulled out his cell phone. Fortunately, its case was waterproof. (It was also acid-proof, fire-proof, and supermonkey-proof. After he got the janitor job, Tom had splurged on a phone case that could handle all of his job-related hazards.)

As the cavemen reached knee-deep water and stood up, rocks in hand, Tom quickly pressed a series of buttons on his phone, then held it up as he cried out:

"BEHOLD MY MIGHTY POWER!"

He'd meant to turn on his phone's emergency strobe while playing the opening bars of Wagner's "Ride of the Valkyries," which was the most fear-inspiring song he could think of. He figured it was the perfect combination of light and sound to amaze and frighten the cavemen into thinking he had magical powers.

Unfortunately, Tom hadn't pressed all the right buttons.

The strobe light began to flash, but instead of "Ride of the Valkyries," his phone started to play the peppy, four-note theme to the *Fruit Fight* game app.

"*Do-dee-doot-doot! Do-dee-doot-doot!*" chirped his phone.

The *Fruit Fight* song did not frighten the cavemen. But it DID confuse them enough to stop and stare at the flashing strobe light in Tom's hand as it bleated out its cheerful ditty.

"*Do-dee-doot-doot! Do-dee-doot-doot!*"

Marisa groaned. "Will you GET A ROCK?!" She'd just found a good-sized one of her own. She cocked her arm back to throw it at the nearest caveman.

But before she could let fly, the caveman screamed.

"TOOKA!"

He pointed in Tom's direction, his eyes as wide as dinner plates.

In an instant, all three cavemen dropped their rocks, turned, and plunged back into the water, fleeing as fast as they could swim.

Tom looked down at his cell phone. "Holy cow! It worked!"

He grinned at Marisa—but she was staring past him, her eyes even bigger and more terrified-looking than the caveman's.

Tom looked back over his shoulder.

A saber-toothed tiger was running down the shore toward them.

T om and Marisa did what anyone else would do in
their shoes: They panicked. With nowhere to run or
hide—there were cliffs on two sides, angry-cavemen-
infested water on the third, and a tiger on the fourth—
they sprinted to the cliff wall and started to climb it.

It was their best option, but it was doomed to fail. The
cliff grew steeper and more sheer as it rose. While they
could climb just high enough to get out of the tiger's
reach, they were bound to get stuck, unable to go anywhere but down.

After that, it was only a matter of time before their
arms would give out and they would fall into the tiger's
waiting jaws.

Nobody knew this better than the tiger. When he saw
the two humans start up the cliff wall, he smiled behind

his huge curved teeth and slowed to a jog. There was no hurry. The humans were trapped, and he was going to enjoy a long, leisurely day of killing and eating them.

He probably wouldn't eat much. He wasn't very hungry. Until all the noise had woken him up, he'd been snoring in his den, sleeping off his full stomach from the human he'd eaten just the day before.

No, this wasn't about food. This was about revenge! How dare they wake him up? All that yelling and rock-throwing. And what was that ear-splitting crash a few minutes ago? It sounded like someone had dropped something extremely heavy off the cliff.

But there was nothing down here now. Just a big, rectangular crater in the mud. Weird.

That wasn't the only weird thing. These humans smelled funny. They weren't like the usual stinky ones he ate, with their body odor and shaggy hair. As these two scrambled in terror up the side of the cliff above him, strange and exotic smells wafted down to him. Since he lived in 10,000 B.C., the tiger had no way of knowing that these scents went by unusual names like "Floral Essence Shampoo" and "Cool Breeze All-Day Deodorant."

He was very curious to find out how these smells tasted.

But not right away. First, he was going to play with his food for a while. It was more fun that way.

The tiger sat back on its haunches and stared up at the doomed humans, clinging terrified to life a few feet above him.

This was turning into a really good day.

🐾 🐾 🐾

"We're stuck," said Marisa. "We can't go any higher."

Tom's arms were already starting to hurt. He looked down at the tiger, sniffing the air and growling just a few feet below them. Then he looked to his right. "We can't go right, either," he said. "There's no handholds over here. What about on your side?"

"There's no way to get past that bush." To Marisa's left, a five-foot-long bush grew out of a crevice in the rock wall. From the way its ripe berries drooped on their stems, Marisa could tell it was too flimsy to use as a handhold. Worse, it was too thick to climb through, too tall to climb above, and impossible to climb below without coming back into eating range of the tiger.

They were definitely stuck.

Then a thought crossed Marisa's mind.

What kind of berries are on that bush?

When she was ten, Marisa had been sent to sleepaway

camp for three weeks. She was terrified of the other campers. They seemed louder, meaner, and even harder to talk to than the kids at her school, who also terrified her. The only way she could avoid them was by keeping her nose buried in a book.

The lone book in their cabin had been *A Field Guide to North American Plant Life*. Over the three weeks, she read it fourteen times. She'd learned an awful lot about plants, but she'd never found any use for all that knowledge. Except for when she occasionally passed a vacant lot and thought to herself, *Somebody should weed that* polygonum cuspidatum *before it takes over the whole block.*

Until now.

"Can you get a hand free?" Marisa asked Tom.

"I'm kind of using both of them?" Tom told her. "Y'know, to keep from falling off the cliff and getting eaten by that tiger?"

"If your life depended on it, could you get a hand free?"

"I guess so."

"Good." Marisa took one hand off the cliff and rummaged in the pocket of her pants. "Hold out your hand," she told him.

Tom did as he was told. Marisa dropped a wrapped sandwich in his open palm.

"You're eating lunch?"

"No! I have a plan. Hold still." With her free hand, Marisa carefully unwrapped the sandwich.

"Why was there a sandwich in your pocket?"

Even clinging to a cliff with one hand, the question was embarrassing enough to make her blush. "I was too nervous to eat before the Show and Tell. This was going to be my celebration sandwich for afterward."

"You know, that solar panel invention was really amazing—"

"Shhhh." Marisa finished unwrapping the sandwich. She pulled off the top slice of rye bread and carefully balanced it next to the rest of the sandwich atop Tom's open palm.

"Don't move," she warned him.

🐾 🐾 🐾

Down below, the tiger suddenly lifted its nose in the air. *What was that smell?*

It was amazing! Mouthwatering! Like some kind of animal flesh that had been cooked in a fire until it was crispy!

Even though his stomach was full, the smell made trickles of drool run down both of his saber teeth.

This day was just getting better and better.

"Can you hurry?" Tom asked. "The tiger is getting riled up. I think it smells the bacon in your sandwich."

"Hang on," said Marisa. She plucked a stem full of berries from the bush and carefully worked the berries off the stem and onto the top layer of avocado on the turkey-bacon-avocado sandwich.

"Are you sure those blueberries are going to go well with the avocado?" Tom asked.

"They're not blueberries," Marisa told him. "They're belladonna."

"Do *those* go well with avocado?"

"Yes and no. They're poisonous."

"We're going to poison ourselves?"

"No. We're going to poison the tiger."

"Oh," Tom thought for a second. "Hey, that's a really good idea!"

Marisa finished loading the sandwich with berries. She carefully placed the slice of rye back on top, then quickly rewrapped the sandwich.

"Can we do this fast?" Tom asked. "I don't know how much longer I can hang on." The tremble in his right arm was turning into a shudder.

"Okay—drop the sandwich."

The tiger couldn't believe his luck. The greatest-smelling thing in the history of the world had just landed at his feet!

He snapped it up in his powerful jaws. Once he chewed past the wrapping paper, it was delicious.

It was more than delicious. It was mind-blowing. Definitely the best thing he'd ever put in his mouth. Even better than baby birds.

And the berries were a great touch. They made a nice, juicy counterpoint to that crispy cooked meat thing.

The tiger chewed and swallowed. It was over all too quickly.

He turned back to the humans. They were still hanging from the cliff. But they were clearly tiring. The one on the right looked like he might fall at any second.

Then the fun would start. Not long now!

Such a great day. Really. And getting better every minute.

Except for that fluttery feeling in his stomach.

❍ ❍ ❍

"How long is this going to take?" Tom asked Marisa.

"I don't know," she replied.

"My arms are shaking. I think I might fall off."

"Try not to fall until the poison kicks in."

"Are you sure belladonna is poisonous to saber-toothed tigers?"

"Not exactly," Marisa admitted. "I've never tried to poison a tiger before."

Something weird was definitely happening in the tiger's stomach.

Not just weird. Painful. It was like a small animal was stuck in there, kicking him from the inside.

The greatest thing he'd ever tasted might not have been so great after all.

He laid down. Maybe he just needed a nap.

No. That wasn't helping. He needed to get up. Move around. Maybe do some stretching.

Nope. Still not helping.

The pain was really . . . getting . . . painful.

Maybe he should throw up.

Yes! Great idea.

Cavemen?! Tigers?! These two have their hands full! Check out page 238.

"He's barfing!" yelled Tom.

"RUN!" screamed Marisa.

They jumped to the ground and sprinted down the shore as fast as their legs would carry them.

The tiger didn't even notice they'd left. He was too busy puking his guts out.

All of a sudden, his day wasn't turning out so great.

W hy . . . are you . . . making us . . . run uphill?"
Tom was panting so hard he could barely get the
words out. They'd run along the lake to where the cliff
gave way to a climbable hillside. Now Marisa was leading
them straight uphill, toward the long ridge where the
cavemen had first thrown rocks at them.

Between pants of her own, she answered the question.
"Got . . . to get . . . to higher ground."

"Why?"

"So next time . . . somebody tries . . . to kill us . . ."—
she took an extra-long pause to gulp more air—"we'll see
them coming."

"Time out!" croaked Tom. He collapsed onto the
ground, although the hill was so steep that he didn't have
to collapse so much as lean forward a little.

Marisa did the same.

"Why do you think somebody's going to try to kill us?" Tom asked.

"Because that's all anybody's done since we got here!"

"But we can't get too far away from where the time machine landed," said Tom, pointing back toward the rocky ledge that was now a few hundred yards below them. "I mean, what if we're not there when they come back for us?"

Marisa shook her head. "Nobody's going to come back for us."

Tom was shocked. "Of course they will!"

She sighed. "No, they won't. They'll never figure out we're here. They'll think you fell into a black hole like the other janitors. And as for me . . ."—she let out a long, pitiful sigh—"they won't even realize I'm gone."

◑ ◓ ◒

Marisa wasn't quite right on either count. Twelve thousand years later at that very moment, Dr. Palindrome stood alone in the CEASE auditorium, examining the solar panel Marisa had used in her Show and Tell.

This really is an amazing invention, he thought to himself. It was a shame that, in all the excitement, the others had forgotten about it. It wasn't as flashy as a time machine. But in its own way, it was revolutionary. It could solve mankind's energy needs! It could save the environment! It could make whoever invented it incredibly rich.

Probably famous, too.

That inventor—the child prodigy he'd hired ten years ago, then forgotten about—what was her name again? Morris? Murphy? Dr. Palindrome felt a pang of jealousy. It had been a long time since his own research had gotten any attention at all. And the director job at CEASE didn't pay very well.

Maybe this Dr. What's-Her-Name could use a business partner. Or a boyfriend—

"Dr. Palindrome?" Dr. Vasquez stood at the door of the auditorium, her face glowing with excitement and post-nacho satisfaction. But when she saw her time machine—with the mud on one side now drying into a hard crust—the glow faded into concern.

"Dr. Vasquez! Congratulations again! What can I do for you?"

"Have you seen Tom Edison? He came back here to clean the time machine, but it's still a mess. And he never showed up at the nacho party. It's very unlike him—we're all a little worried he might've met with a . . . janitor accident."

"That IS worrying," Dr. Palindrome agreed. Janitor accidents meant a lot of paperwork for him. And finding replacements was getting to be a nightmare. "I'll check the footage from the security cameras."

◑ ◐ ◓

Minutes later, Dr. Palindrome sat alone in his office, staring in disbelief at the security camera footage of Marisa and Tom entering the time machine . . . followed by the time machine's disappearance . . . followed by its reappearance ten seconds later, with nobody inside it.

I must tell Dr. Vasquez immediately!

He sprang up from his chair and started toward the door.

But then he stopped.

He thought about it some more.

Losing the janitor would be a shame. Everybody seemed to like that one, and they were a real pain to replace. Still, mysterious janitor disappearances were common as dirt around CEASE.

And if that solar panel scientist disappeared, and nobody went looking for her, what would happen to those solar panels? And all the money and fame that went along with them?

Hmmmm . . .

Dr. Palindrome sat back down at his desk and rewound the only evidence on Earth of Tom and Marisa's disappearance.

His office door opened a crack. Dr. Vasquez poked her head in.

"Any sign of Tom on the security cameras?"

Dr. Palindrome clicked the "ERASE VIDEO" button, then gave Dr. Vasquez a look of thoughtful concern.

"None at all. It's a real mystery."

Oh, THAT is evil, Dr. P! See page 242.

O ther than Dr. Palindrome, only three people in all of human history knew what had happened to Tom and Marisa.

Their names were Dug, Edd, and Jim. They were the cavemen who'd spent the past hour trying to kill the two strangers who'd literally appeared out of nowhere. And at that very moment, exactly twelve thousand years before Dr. Palindrome erased the video, Dug, Edd, and Jim were standing on the narrow ledge where the time machine had first materialized.

JIM   DUG   EDD

They stared down in disbelief at the vomiting saber-toothed tiger a hundred feet below them.

"Mugga Tooka dugga," said Edd.

Roughly translated, this meant, *"This is really quite shocking. I've never seen anyone escape Tooka the Tiger. And they didn't just escape—they left Tooka barfing his guts out! That's a heck of a thing."*

"Durrr?" asked Jim.

In that context, "durrr" meant: *"Whaddaya make of this, Dug? Wild stuff, huh? What's your take on it?"*

Edd and Jim waited nervously for Dug's answer. Dug was the leader of their whole clan, because he was the strongest, the smartest, and the most likely to bash your brains in with a rock if you disagreed with him.

Dug thought for a long time before answering. Finally, he spoke.

"Hurg blurg 'do-dee-doot-doot' urg Tooka nugurg."

And by that, Dug meant: *"Let's review the facts here, gentlemen. We're standing atop that ridge above us, innocently gathering rocks as we do. Out of nowhere, a giant magic box appears, right on this very ledge! Which I think we can all agree is a highly unusual situation.*

"We follow standard procedure—huck some rocks at it, roll a boulder down the hill—and suddenly, two strange humans

pop out of the magic box! Which, again—is HIGHLY unusual. A magic box is one thing. But a magic box that gives birth to strangers? We're definitely in uncharted territory here.

"Then it gets weirder. The magic box disappears! And leaves the strangers behind! Now, as your leader, I have to admit—at this point, I probably should've taken a step back and done some strategic analysis. But there was a lot of stuff happening at once, it was very stressful, and I figured, let's just run the usual playbook. Which is, y'know, 'Strangers are invading our territory, let's kill them with rocks.'

"Makes perfect sense in most situations.

"But this was NOT a normal situation. Because the second we get within rock-throwing range, Stranger Guy pulls out a MAGIC ROCK! I've never seen anything like it. Those flashing lights! And that sound—'do-dee-doot-doot!' What IS that? It's as irritating as it is catchy. Honestly, even if I never hear it again, it's going to take me days to get that sound out of my head.

"Mark my words, gentlemen—that magic rock is the key to understanding this whole thing.

"So Stranger Guy's waving it around, and Stranger Lady seems mad about it. Which makes NO sense at all. Why get mad at the guy with the magic rock when he's on your side? For the life of me, I can't figure out where Stranger Lady fits into all of this.

"But let's just put a pin in that and move on—because then *Tooka shows up! And I'm thinking, A) FINALLY, something normal happens, B) we gotta get outta here pronto or we're gonna get eaten, and C) magic rock or not, those strangers are tiger food.*

"But C) turns out to be dead wrong. By the time we get back up here and take a look around, Tooka's drowning in his own puke, and the strangers are running up the hillside over there.

"When you add it all up, I think it's pretty obvious what's going on here and what we need to do next. Follow me."

Dug started up the hill toward Marisa and Tom. Nodding in agreement, Edd and Jim followed.

◐ ◑ ◒

"Don't you think we've got enough rocks?" Tom asked Marisa. They were on top of the high ridge above the lake. Marisa was frantically piling the rocks they'd already gathered into a makeshift barricade.

"There's no such thing as 'enough rocks!'" she told him. "Rocks are everything in this world! They're weapons. They're building materials. They're probably money! From now on, our lives depend on rocks! We've got to keep gathering them!"

"Geez," muttered Tom. "You're acting like we're going to be stuck here forever."

"We ARE stuck here forever!" Marisa was sure of this.

"No, we're not!" Tom was every bit as sure of that. "Dr. Vasquez and the others are going to come back for us! It's just going to take them awhile to figure out we're gone."

Marisa rolled her eyes. "Tom, they have a time machine. It can come back to any time in history. Including ten minutes ago. If they were coming back for us, they'd already be here."

"Yeah, but . . . I mean . . . it's like . . . uhhh . . . " Tom tried to understand the logic of what Marisa was saying. Thinking about it made his head hurt.

Finally, he gave up. "Whatever. I don't know time machines. But I know people. And there's no way Dr. Vasquez would abandon her fellow scientists like that."

"You're not a scientist," Marisa reminded him. "You're a janitor."

Tom looked hurt. "I'm not just any janitor," he said in a wounded voice. "I'm a scientist-janitor. Everybody knows that."

Marisa opened her mouth to tell Tom he was wrong— that what everybody except him actually knew was that he'd been duped into taking a life-threatening job that nobody else wanted. And that the only person who thought Tom was an actual scientist was Tom.

But when she saw the look on his face, Marisa couldn't bear to tell him the truth. "Just get more rocks," she said again as she turned back to her barricade-building. "The next people who climb that hill are going to try to kill us, and it'd be a whole lot better if we killed them first."

"Do-dee-doot-doot!"

Marisa looked up. "What did you say?"

"I didn't say anything," Tom told her. "They did."

Marisa poked her head up over the pile of rocks and looked in the direction Tom was pointing.

Down the hill a hundred yards below them were Dug, Edd, and Jim.

"Do-dee-doot-doot," Dug yelled. Then all three cavemen fell to their knees, raised their hands in the air, and bowed down to them.

"Do-dee-doot-doot," they chanted.

Tom looked at Marisa. "If they're still trying to kill us, that's a really weird way to do it."

Marisa had to agree.

Talking to strangers—or anybody, really—had always been scary and stressful for Marisa. It was even more stressful trying to talk to strangers who couldn't seem to decide whether they wanted to murder her or worship her. Especially when they didn't know any words in English except for "do-dee-doot-doot," which technically was not even a word.

Marisa opened her mouth to speak, but nothing came out. Fortunately, Tom spoke up for both of them.

"Me Tom," he said, pointing to himself. "She Marisa."

The cavemen looked confused.

"Don't use pronouns," Marisa told Tom. "They won't understand."

"Tom," said Tom, pointing to himself.

"Marisa," she managed to say, pointing to herself.

"Do-dee-doot-doot," said Dug.

"Do-dee-doot-doot," agreed Edd and Jim.

"Whaddaya think that means?" Tom asked Marisa.

"It's the sound your phone made."

"Oooooh . . . *Now* I get it!"

The cavemen were slowly getting to their feet. When Tom pulled out his phone, they froze. And when he turned the strobe light on and opened the *Fruit Fight* game, they fell to their knees again and began to bow, chanting "do-dee-doot-doot" along with the theme song.

Tom was thrilled. "Wowzers! It's just like on *Star Trip*!"

"Turn it off!" Marisa warned him.

"Why?"

"If the whole reason they're not killing us is your phone, we have to make sure the battery doesn't run out. How much have you got left?"

Tom checked his phone display. "Sixty-eight percent."

"Switch it to low power, shut off the Wi-Fi, close all your apps, and turn on Airplane Mode."

"What if somebody tries to call me?"

Marisa's jaw dropped. "Are you serious? Have you *ever* gotten a phone call from the future?"

"No. But I've also never been stuck in the past."

"Just close everything!" Marisa turned to look at the cavemen, who were nervously poking their heads back up from the ground. "Now what?"

Tom thought about it. "Why don't we ask them where we can get a bite to eat? I haven't had anything since lunch. And that was, like, minus twelve thousand years ago."

Marisa nodded. She was even hungrier than Tom, because she'd used her lunch to poison a saber-toothed tiger. "Good idea. Ask them about food."

Tom stood in front of the cavemen, pointed to his mouth, and said, "Food."

They looked up at him, confused.

"Food?" he repeated.

"Foo-dee-food-food?" Dug asked.

"Foo-dee-food-food!" Edd and Jim chanted.

Marisa sighed. This was going to take awhile.

🐾🐾🐾

An hour later, after endless rounds of sign language, miming, and so many repetitions of the *Fruit Fight* theme song that the phone's battery life fell to 62 percent, the cavemen agreed to take Tom and Marisa to a place where they could eat.

Before they left the hillside, Tom insisted on arranging

a series of rocks into a giant sign just above the spot where the time machine had landed. It read:

WE WENT THAT WAY ➡
BACK SOON! DON'T LEAVE!

"I hope Dr. Vasquez doesn't come back for us in the middle of the night," Tom said. "She might not see the sign."

"Don't worry about it," said Marisa. She was too tired and hungry to start another argument by trying to convince Tom that nobody was coming back for them.

As the sun began to set, they followed the cavemen off the hill and into the woods away from the lake.

With Dug in the lead, the cavemen led Tom and Marisa into the forest, to a wide clearing the size of a football field with the mouth of a cave at the far end. At the cave entrance, they could see a fire burning.

"Hey, look at that," said Tom as they approached the entrance. "They actually DO live in a cave."

Marisa didn't answer, because she was very busy trying not to fall into a giant hole that had just appeared out of nowhere.

"Look out!"

It was a three-foot-wide, ten-foot-deep pit about twenty yards in front of the cave entrance.

"What do you think that's for?" Tom asked.

Marisa shrugged. "Self-defense?"

They followed the cavemen into the cave, skirting the edge of the fire. Their curiosity about the pit was instantly replaced by a much more immediate question: *What on earth was that horrible smell?*

It was like a combination of sewage, body odor, and dead animals.

But mostly sewage.

"Oh, geez," said Tom, putting his hands in front of his nose. "That's powerful stuff." The smell was so bad that he and Marisa barely even noticed all the bats flitting in and out of an unseen lair at the back of the cave.

Neither the bats nor the smell seemed to bother the forty cavemen, cavewomen, and cavechildren who were sitting in a big semicircle around the fire.

But the sight of Tom and Marisa DID bother them, quite a bit. When the two strangers appeared in the fire-light, the cavepeople all gasped and leaped to their feet. A few shrieked in fear. Cavepeople, it seemed, were even more terrified of strangers than Marisa was—and strangers inside their cave was a real crisis.

Moving quickly, one of the younger, stronger-looking men picked up a wooden club and charged straight at Tom, screaming as he went.

Tom froze in terror. No one had ever run screaming at him with a club before, and he didn't know how to react.

Fortunately, as the club-wielding man rushed past Dug, the clan leader stuck his foot out and tripped him. The club went flying, and the man did a face-plant. He wound up spread-eagled on the ground in front of Tom.

Tom and Marisa both gasped. So did most of the cavepeople.

Dug put his foot firmly on the man's back and yelled, "Oooga magook do-dee-doot-doot Tooka looga!"

Everyone except Tom and Marisa understood what Dug meant, which was: *"First of all, Gary, I'm sorry I had to get rough with you. But I'm your leader, it's my job, and I don't know how many times I've warned you about your poor impulse control. Once you get out from under my foot, I want to speak to you privately, maybe talk about getting you some counseling.*

"Second, and more importantly—I know all of you are wondering what these strangers with weird clothes are doing in our cave, and why Stranger Guy here has no eyebrows.

"I have no idea about the eyebrows. That's a mystery.

But here's what I do know: Stranger Guy has a magic rock. It goes 'do-dee-doot-doot.' Somehow, he used this magic rock to defeat Tooka. It was the craziest thing I've ever seen. One minute, Tooka's about to eat them. The next minute, he's puking his guts out.

"This is a game-changer, people. Seriously. I don't think it's a stretch to say this magic rock situation is going to require us to fundamentally rethink a lot of our assumptions about the way the world works.

"And there are things we still don't know. For one thing, Stranger Guy's got the magic rock, but it doesn't seem to stop Stranger Lady from yelling at him. What's the deal with their relationship? Does she have a magic rock, too? Why does she keep getting mad at him?

"I don't have answers yet. But in the short term, I don't want us getting sideways with Stranger Guy and Stranger Lady. Let's just assume they're supernatural beings with the power to make us double over barfing like they did to Tooka, and let's open our cave to them and give them all our food so they don't hurt us. Okay? Everybody clear on that? Good.

"Oh! One more thing. I have no idea why they're both holding their noses and looking totally grossed out. That's new. They weren't doing it a minute ago."

"Other than the smell, this seems like a pretty great situation," Tom said. "We've got the best seats in the cave, and they gave us all their food."

Tom and Marisa were sitting at the edge of the fire, as close as possible to the cave entrance so they could avoid the worst of the stench. In front of them was a good-sized pile of berries and nuts. The entire clan stared at them in silence, waiting for Tom and Marisa to eat.

Marisa shook her head. "This isn't good. It's terrible."

"Because of the bats?" They'd both been smacked in the head by the wings of the low-flying bats that were constantly flitting in and out of the cave.

"It's not the bats. It's everything else. First of all, I think they're using the back of the cave as a toilet. That doesn't just make it smell bad—it spreads disease. Second, look how skinny these people are!"

Tom looked at the group. "They *are* a lot skinnier than I expected cavepeople to be. Those *Flintstones* cartoons were really misleading."

"You know why they're so skinny? Because they don't have enough food! These people are barely surviving as hunter-gatherers. We've got to teach them agriculture. And basic hygiene. And fast—if they're going to make it through the next winter, they've got to start planting food *now.*"

Tom thought about it for a moment. "I dunno. Seems like an awful lot to explain. They probably won't like it. And if we're only here for a little while—"

"Tom! We're going to be here *forever.* If we don't help them now, we'll starve, too!"

Tom sighed but didn't say anything. They were just going to have to agree to disagree about whether they'd be rescued.

"I think we should share this food with them," Marisa added. "They look so hungry."

"Good idea," agreed Tom. As they both stood up to share the pile of fruit and nuts with the others, Marisa grabbed Tom's arm.

"Wait! There's one more thing I'm worried about— that tiger."

"What about it?"

"If the berries didn't kill it, it'll come back. We've got to figure out how to protect ourselves. And them, too," she added, gesturing to the clan.

"Relax," said Tom. "These people have it all worked out. Look at that painting."

He pointed at the wall across from them. Just visible in the flickering firelight was a crude but unmistakable charcoal drawing of a saber-toothed tiger. In front of the giant tiger were a couple dozen faceless, stick-figure humans about the size of chipmunks. All the humans had their arms raised over their heads.

"See?" Tom said to Marisa. "All the humans are jumping up and down and cheering, like, 'Yay! We beat the giant tiger!' Or maybe it's, 'Yay! We love the giant tiger!'"

Marisa stared at the painting for a moment. "*Or,*" she said, "they're running away and screaming. Like, 'Eeeek! The tiger's chasing us!'"

Tom looked closer at the painting, then frowned. "Oh, yeah. I guess it could go either way. We should teach these guys how to draw better stick figures. Either way, though, I wouldn't sweat it. If they hadn't figured out how to handle the tiger, they all would've been eaten by now. Maybe this fire's all the protection they need."

Marisa had to admit Tom's logic made more sense than usual. But as she scooped up a handful of nuts and berries and started to hand them out to the confused but grateful cavepeople, she couldn't help glancing from the cave painting to the fire to the darkness beyond the entrance, wondering where that tiger was . . . and how soon it'd be back.

That same moment, a little over a mile away, the tiger lay flat on his belly in the tall grass near his lair. Unlike the cavepeople, he kept his lair very clean, so he didn't want to return to it until he was finished being sick. And he wasn't anywhere near finished yet.

It had been a terrible day. But in between retches, he cheered himself up by thinking about the future.

As soon as he recovered, he was going to find those two humans—the ones who smelled like Floral Essence and Cool Breeze All Day. Then he was going to sink his teeth into them and find out exactly what those smells tasted like.

And he'd do it in his favorite way—slowly, with shrieks of agony that lasted for hours.

He was really going to enjoy that.

But first, he had to throw up again.

Lots of sights, sounds, and smells in that cave! See page 244.

Early the next afternoon, Marisa stood in the middle of a wide rectangle of freshly plowed soil at the bottom of the big clearing below the cave. Using a three-foot-long stick, she carefully poked a long, straight row of holes in the soil.

Dug, Edd, Jim, and half a dozen other cavemen sat on the ground just outside the plowed area, watching Marisa with looks of anger and confusion.

The anger was mostly because that soil hadn't plowed itself. The cavemen had done it on Marisa's orders, using a combination of flat rocks and their fingers. It had been hard, dirty work.

The confusion was because they had no idea why they'd done it, or why Marisa was poking holes in the newly upturned ground.

Tom sat by the edge of the group, tossing pebbles at a little hoop he'd made using a flexible tree branch. He understood exactly what Marisa was trying to do. Even so, it was slow, boring stuff and no fun to watch.

Marisa finished poking the row of holes. She held up a handful of seeds.

"Seeds," she said.

The cavemen just stared at her. Tom tossed another pebble through his hoop.

"Seeds," she said again, louder and more confidently. She'd been lecturing the cavemen about the life-or-death issues of good hygiene and agriculture for seven straight hours now. She was going hoarse from the effort, but it had done wonders for overcoming her fear of talking to strangers.

She was so pleased about this, and about the progress she was making to help the tribe, that she barely noticed how annoyed the cavemen were getting.

"Seeds," they all repeated back to her in dull, sullen voices.

Marisa went down the row, putting seeds in the holes. "Seeds. Plant. Ground. Grow. Food," she said.

The first three hours of her lecture had been a

language lesson. She hoped it had sunk in and the cave-men understood her.

It hadn't, and they didn't.

Instead, they all looked at Dug, their leader. Dug just shrugged. Then he turned to watch Tom toss a pebble at the little hoop, which was much more interesting to him than this poking-holes-in-the-ground business.

With the seeds now planted, Marisa walked over to where a large, thick leaf held a very unpleasant item she'd retrieved earlier from the back of the cave. She carefully picked up the leaf.

"Fertilizer," she said.

The cavemen just stared at her.

She tried a simpler word. "Poop?" She moved closer to show the men the contents of the leaf.

They looked horrified.

"I know!" she said, scrunching up her face in a pained look. "Gross. But food! For plants."

She picked up a short stick and carefully added small dollops of poop to the holes, then covered them with dirt. When she was finished, she put down her stick tools and her leaf full of poop and tried to sum up the entire crop cycle using big, exaggerated hand gestures.

"So . . . Seeds. Ground. Plant. Poop. Sun. Rain. Time. Grow. Food. Eat! Live! Good! Understand?"

The cavemen did not understand.

Dug raised his hand. "Marsha?" he asked.

"Marisa," she corrected him.

"Marsha."

She sighed. It was hard to tell whether the cavemen couldn't pronounce her name or just didn't want to. "Yes, Dug?"

"Marsha uga tuga skooga Tom alooga," said Dug.

Marisa had no idea what he meant by that. But the cavemen all did, and roughly speaking, it was this: *"I have to be completely honest here, Marsha: This is ridiculous. First you spend three hours trying to teach us your language—which is very patronizing, because hello? There are more of us than there are of you! Why aren't YOU learning OUR language?*

"Then you spend another two hours yelling at us about— and correct me if I'm wrong here, but this was my takeaway— how we're not supposed to poop in the back of the cave anymore? Which makes no sense at all! What are we supposed to do, go off in the woods somewhere? Even in the winter? When it's cold out? Personally, I don't see the point.

"But then you drag us out here and take it to a whole other level of crazy. You make us dig up all this ground for no reason

at all. *Then you pick up some poop from the cave—which might be okay where you come from, but around here, that's disgusting—and you put the poop in tiny holes in the ground? On top of a bunch of perfectly good seeds? That we could have eaten instead? Seriously?*

"I mean, seriously?

"Marsha, take a step back and think about what you're doing here. This is really not normal. Personally, I'm starting to think you're either a witch or you're mentally ill. Either way, I don't know why Tom puts up with it. If I weren't so worried about him destroying us with his magic rock, we'd be having a whole other conversation right now. And trust me when I say you wouldn't like it.

"You want to keep poking your little poop holes in the ground? Do what you have to. But I'm out. If you need me, I'll be over here, tossing pebbles through this hoop thing that Tom made. Which is a LOT more fun than whatever it is you're doing."

Marisa watched with concern as first Dug and then the rest of the cavemen turned their attention away from her and toward Tom and the silly little pebble game he was playing.

"Tom, can I talk to you for a second? Privately?"

"Sure thing." Tom got up and walked over to Marisa.

When he did, the cavemen eagerly took over his pebble-throwing.

"Can you stop doing that pebble thing? It's really distracting."

"I know. Sorry! But look at them—they're really enjoying it."

"They have to learn how to plant crops! It's a matter of life and death! I'm trying to save all our lives here!"

"I know! But it's been, like, seven straight hours of trying to save our lives. And we're all getting a little antsy. I think we need a study break."

"A study break? Seriously?"

"Yes! Seriously! Marisa, what you're doing is awesome and totally helpful—but you're pushing them too hard."

"Why do you say that?" The thought hadn't occurred to Marisa. From her point of view, all she was doing was trying to help them.

"I can just tell," said Tom. "Look, why don't we do this pebble thing for a few minutes? Let them blow off some steam. Then we'll come back fresh. Okay?"

"What IS that pebble thing, anyway?"

"I don't even know. It's just a game I made up to pass the time. But they're really into it. I'm thinking I should expand it a little. Add some rules. Maybe use bigger rocks."

Marisa watched Dug toss a pebble that just missed the hoop. The other cavemen groaned in disappointment. Then two of them scrambled to fetch the pebble while a third, pebble in hand, lined up his own shot.

She sighed. "Okay, fine. You play the pebble game for a while. I'll just be over here, solving our starvation problem all by myself. No big deal."

"Awesome! Thanks!" Tom trotted off to rejoin the cavemen.

I was being sarcastic! Marisa thought.

She went back to poking holes in the ground. As she bent over the stick, she realized something:

We haven't talked about the tiger problem yet.

She resolved to make tiger defense the subject of her next lesson. Which would start just as soon as they got tired of that silly pebble game.

Twenty-four hours later, Tom and the cavemen still hadn't gotten tired of the silly pebble game.

In fact, they were obsessed with it.

Thanks to Tom's creative rule-making and the cavemen's excitement at having discovered organized sports, the game had become much bigger, more complicated, and infinitely more dangerous than just tossing pebbles through a hoop. It was now a full-court combination of basketball, bowling, and martial arts that Tom had named Rockball.

Most of the clearing—excluding the still-mysterious open pit and Marisa's plot of farmland—was now one giant Rockball court, with rocks whizzing through the air every which way whenever a game was in progress. For most of the day, the games had been nonstop.

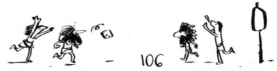

Tom had split the men of the clan into teams, and they were in the middle of a round-robin tournament.

Marisa was not happy about any of this.

"Tom! We have to talk!"

"Can it wait? I'm playing here!"

"What's more important—the game? Or the fact that a saber-toothed tiger could stroll in here and eat one of us at any minute?"

"Relax! If these guys aren't worried, I don't think we should be, either."

"Oh, sure. Because the people who poop where they sleep NEVER make bad choices."

"Are you being sarcastic?"

"YES! Please, Tom. You have to help me talk to Dug about this. I have a plan for defending us against a tiger attack. But I need help!"

Tom sighed. "Do you have to talk to Dug right this minute? His team is on deck. And he doesn't like to be bothered before a big game."

"Please! I'm begging you! Our lives are at stake here!"

Tom thought that was a little exaggerated. But he nodded. "Okay. Just as soon as somebody scores a header."

Twenty yards downfield, a caveman hurled a rock at

a second caveman's head. It bounced off his skull with a dull *thunk*, knocking him out cold.

"There we go." Tom stepped onto the field waving his hands and making a "T" sign. "Time out! Marisa talk!"

The cavemen all groaned. Marisa hurried across the field to Dug, who glared at her.

"Dug. Problem! Tooka." It was the one word in the caveman language she was sure she understood.

Dug shrugged. "Tooka?"

"Tooka. Eat. Us!" Marisa pantomimed a tiger eating a human.

Dug nodded. "Tooka eat us."

Marisa's eyes widened. They understood each other! This was real progress.

"Danger," said Marisa. "Tooka eat us! Must protect!"

Dug's eyebrows scrunched up a little. He wasn't quite following her.

Marisa pointed to the ten-foot-deep pit. "Idea. Tooka. Pit. Trap."

Dug un-scrunched his eyebrows and nodded. "Tooka. Pit. Trap."

Marisa beamed. Were they on the same wavelength? She headed over to the pit, beckoning Dug to follow. He rolled his eyes, but reluctantly joined her at the edge of the pit.

Marisa pointed at the bottom of the pit, ten feet below them. "Sharp. Stakes." She pantomimed driving stakes into the ground inside the pit. "Cover. Pit. Branches, leaves?" She pantomimed spreading things over the pit to hide the hole. "Decoy. Bait?" She gestured to the far side of the pit. "Tooka. Run. Fall. Pit. Stakes. Sharp. Die." She pantomimed the tiger falling into the pit and getting impaled on the stakes. Understand?"

Dug nodded. "Tooka. Pit."

Marisa was thrilled. They understood each other!

"Great! So . . . Get stakes! Sharpen!" She pantomimed gathering wood, then sharpening an edge. "Yes? Help?"

Dug frowned and shook his head. "Rockball."

The n he turned around and walked away.

Marisa's shoulders sagged in defeat. Tom tried to cheer her up. "I think he got what you were saying, though. That's a plus, right?"

"He definitely made the connection between Tooka and the pit. Maybe that's why they dug it in the first place—to trap Tooka. But it's too shallow. If Tooka fell in, he'd just jump out again. So we need to put sharp stakes in the bottom. And I need the cavemen to help me find wood for the stakes. And then sharpen the ends."

"That's going to be tough. They kind of just want to play Rockball right now."

"But this is urgent! We have to make a tiger trap NOW. Could you use your phone on them? Please? If you flash the lights and play the do-dee-doot-doot music, they'll pay attention."

Tom grimaced. "There's kind of a problem with that."

"What is it?"

"My battery died."

"WHAT?! How? Last night, it was at 40 percent!"

"I know. But I got up early, and there was nothing to do, so I thought I'd play a little *Fruit Fight.* Y'know, just to kill some time until everybody woke up—"

"ARE YOU KIDDING ME?!"

All the cavemen turned to stare at Tom and Marisa. She lowered her voice.

"Tom! That phone was everything! It was the only reason they didn't kill us!"

"I know! But things are different now. I taught them Rockball! And I'm, like, the fourth best player in the clan. So I think we're in a pretty good place. Although you should probably stop yelling at them about stuff. 'Cause I don't think that's going over too well. They're getting a little mad at you."

"ROCKBALL!" Dug yelled at Tom from across the field. The cavemen were impatient for the game to start again.

"I gotta get back to the game," Tom told Marisa. "Are you cool with finding the wood and sharpening the stakes yourself for a while? I'll help you as soon as my team gets knocked out of the tournament. Okay?"

Marisa looked horrified. "Tom, this is life or death—"

"It's probably not, though! Don't worry! We're going to be fine!"

Tom gave her an upbeat smile, but when he turned away from her to go back to the game, the smile faded. In spite of himself, he was starting to get concerned. It had been almost two whole days. Why hadn't they been rescued by now?

Wherever you are, Dr. Vasquez, Tom said to himself, *please stop and think about me and Marisa. And come back for us.*

At that very moment, exactly twelve thousand years later, Dr. Vasquez actually WAS thinking about Tom. In fact, everyone at CEASE was thinking about him.

Unfortunately, that was because they were holding his memorial service in the cafeteria. Shortly after Dr. Palindrome's review of the building's security cameras found nothing (at least, according to Dr. Palindrome), yet another mini black hole showed up in Dr. Palavi's office. This led everyone to conclude the worst: that Tom had suffered the same fate as so many CEASE janitors before him.

Dr. Vasquez stood at a podium, next to a large framed portrait of a smiling Tom in his janitor outfit. Her fingernails were painted a somber black to match her dress, and her voice quivered with emotion as she spoke to the mournful crowd of fellow scientists (plus Doris the receptionist, who had taken the news especially hard).

"There will never be another janitor who touches our lives like Tom Edison did," Dr. Vasquez declared. "There was nobody on earth more fun to be around, more knowledgeable about *Star Trip* trivia, or more dedicated to the pursuit of science—even when he didn't really understand any of it."

She turned to Tom's portrait and spoke to it as if Tom himself were standing there. "Buddy, if I could fly my time machine into that black hole and bring you back, I would. But black holes don't work that way. And that's why today, there's a black hole in my heart.

"But from now on, your portrait will hang in the CEASE hall of fame—the only nonscientist of below-average intelligence who we've ever honored in this way. And alongside your portrait, in memory of all those Stump the Janitor games we enjoyed, I'm going to personally hang this vintage *Star Trip* poster."

She reached under the podium and pulled out a framed original poster for *Star Trip II: Excelsior's Revenge*, widely considered to be the best of the *Star Trip* movie adaptations.

"I bought this on eBay just for you, Tom. It was surprisingly expensive. But you're worth it. Tomorrow morning, we're holding a press conference to announce my time machine invention to the world. I wish you could be there. But since you can't, I'm dedicating it to you. From now on, I'm not going to think of it as a time machine, but as a TOM machine. Informally, of course. I don't really expect other people to call it that. It'd be very confusing for them. But in my heart, it'll always be a Tom machine. Good-bye, friend."

The scientists applauded wildly as Dr. Vasquez left the podium. Then Dr. Overtree got up to speak.

"There's SO MUCH I want to say about Tom Edison. First of all—"

WWHHHHZZZZZZHHHHHHH!

Dr. Overtree's words were drowned out by the deafening white noise of an industrial-strength floor buffer. All the scientists turned in their chairs to see the new janitor, Jason, pushing the massive machine across the floor at the back of the room.

Jason had started work the day before, and he had very strong opinions about what the janitor job involved. Many of these opinions were not shared by the CEASE staff. But because he was the only person Dr. Palindrome could find to do the job—and because he was six-foot-five, rippling with muscles, and enjoyed showing off the tattoos he'd gotten while in prison—the scientists hadn't yet found a way to successfully challenge Jason's opinions.

Even so, interrupting Tom's memorial service with an industrial floor buffer was a bit much. Several of the scientists stood and waved their arms in the air, trying to catch Jason's attention.

"Excuse me. EXCUSE ME!" Dr. Overtree bravely placed himself in the path of the floor buffer, forcing Jason to stop the machine.

"Dude. I'm buffing here."

"Which we appreciate! We do. But we're holding a memorial service for our departed friend. It's a highly emotional and deeply important—"

"Buddy," Jason talked over him. "We got rules here! Floor gets buffed at three. No exceptions."

"I'm sorry, whose rules are these?"

"THIS GUY'S." Jason put up a massive fist, thumb out, and pointed at himself. "Take a hike. Cafeteria's closed. You don't have to go home, but you can't stay here."

Everyone looked at Dr. Palindrome, who shrugged meekly. Disappointed but unwilling to challenge a man who weighed twice as much as they did and had a long criminal record, the scientists began to file out of the room.

"Take your chairs with you!" Jason yelled at them. "Your mom doesn't work here! Gotta clean up after yourselves."

Dr. Salaam bravely piped up. "Excuse me, but technically speaking, isn't cleaning up a janitor's job—"

WWHHHHZZZZZZHHHHHH! Dr. Salaam was no match for the floor buffer.

♦ ♦ ♦

Moments later, as the scientists milled about the hallway, carrying chairs they weren't quite sure what to do with, Dr. Vasquez approached Dr. Palindrome.

"Excuse me, Doctor—"

"Yes, Doctor! May I just say, that was a wonderful tribute to Tom. And I'm SO looking forward to your press conference tomorrow! It's going to be SUCH a thrill to see you instantly become the most famous scientist in the world. What an invention!"

"Thank you so much! But speaking of inventions, I was wondering something."

"Yes?"

"The scientist who did that Show and Tell right before me—Marina, was it?"

"Marisa, actually. Marisa Morice." Dr. Palindrome had no trouble at all remembering Marisa's name, because he'd spent the past two days carefully erasing it from every notebook, document, and patent application in her lab, then writing the name "Emo R. Palindrome" in its place.

"I've been trying to track her down to invite her to lunch," said Dr. Vasquez. "I thought her solar panel invention was brilliant, and I wanted to apologize for spoiling her announcement with my time machine."

"That is SO very kind of you! But unfortunately, Dr. Morice is no longer working at CEASE."

"Really? Where did she go? And did she take her invention with her?"

"It's a rather long story." And one that Dr. Palindrome had spent hours carefully making up. "You see, the solar panel project was actually mine. Dr. Morice really wasn't much more than a glorified lab assistant. But I offered to give her all the credit for the invention because, well, to be honest, she had absolutely nothing else going on in her life. No friends or family—did you know she was an orphan? Very sad story."

That part of Dr. Palindrome's story was actually true. Marisa WAS an orphan. The rest of it was nonsense, especially what came next:

"I thought I was doing her a favor by giving her all the credit," Dr. Palindrome continued. "But she was racked with guilt over it. And after the Show and Tell, she decided she couldn't live a lie, no matter how much fame or money it might bring her. So she left the next day to join a Buddhist monastery in the Himalayas, where she plans to spend the rest of her life in silent meditation."

"That is the strangest story I've ever heard," said Dr. Vasquez.

Dr. Palindrome nodded enthusiastically. "It really is! It's very, VERY strange." But unlike the other stories he'd considered making up to explain Dr. Morice's disappearance—fatal car accident, incurable disease, legal problems involving an international car theft ring that she'd masterminded, etc.—the Buddhist monastery story was almost impossible to disprove.

"So then . . . the solar panel invention was yours?" Dr. Vasquez asked.

"That's correct," said Dr. Palindrome. "I'll be announcing it in a week or two, once all the hoopla has settled down after your big time machine announcement."

"Well, then congratulations!" said Dr. Vasquez. "And thank you SO MUCH for solving mankind's energy needs in an environmentally friendly way! That is amazing. I do feel bad about Marisa—we seemed to have so much in common, and I was hoping we'd become friends. But I'm really looking forward to seeing you get all the credit for the invention. Not to mention the money. I'm sure it'll make you fantastically wealthy."

"Fingers crossed!" said Dr. Palindrome with a smile.

Then he excused himself and went back to his office to finish erasing Marisa's name from her life's work.

B ack in the Stone Age, the next morning dawned bright and sunny. It was perfect weather for the finals of the Rockball tournament. The entire clan gathered along the sides of the clearing to watch Dug's team play Edd's team in human history's first organized sports championship.

Edd and his teammates were a little nervous. Since Rockball had only existed for two days, and this was the first-ever tournament final, they still had some unanswered questions about the rules.

Their biggest question was this: If you beat the clan leader's team in the finals, will he kill everyone on your team?

No one could say for sure. They couldn't ask Dug himself, because they didn't want to give him ideas. They'd tried to ask Tom, who'd not only taught them the game, but also was refereeing the final after his own team had been knocked out in the semis. But unfortunately, Tom didn't understand a word of what they were asking.

Ultimately, Edd and his team decided it might be wise to lose the game, just in case.

Meanwhile, the only person in the clan who wasn't playing, refereeing, or watching the final was Marisa. She'd spent the rest of the previous day scouring the forest for tree branches that were exactly the right size for sharpening into tiger-trap stakes. Then, after the rest of the tribe had gone to sleep, she'd stayed up until dawn using a rock to sharpen one of the branches into a stake.

Marisa had meant to sharpen a dozen of them, but using a rock to sharpen a tree branch turned out to be long, slow, painfully difficult work. In ten straight hours of sharpening, she'd only managed to finish one stake. In fact, it was only her years of experience working long, slow, painfully difficult hours alone in her lab that had given her the strength and focus to do that much.

Now she was exhausted, frustrated, and bleeding from several blisters on her hands. Taking her one sharpened stake with her, she went to join the others at the Rockball final, hoping that when the game ended, she could finally get help sharpening the other stakes and fixing them in the ground at the bottom of the pit.

For the life of her, Marisa couldn't understand why no one else was worried about defending themselves against that tiger. How much more time did they have before it came back? She had a nagging feeling that it could show up at any minute.

♤ ♧ ♡

Marisa was right. At that very moment, Tooka the tiger was emerging from his lair. After two full days of sleeping off his berry poisoning, he was finally ready to eat again.

As he took a long, lazy stretch in the morning sun, he wondered who he'd end up eating first. The human who smelled of Floral Essence? Or the other one, Cool Breeze All Day?

Of course, the cavemen might offer him a different choice of meal. He'd been eating members of their clan for a long time now, and they'd worked out a pretty good system for deciding on the menu. But Tooka had already made up his mind.

He was going to have his dinner and his revenge all at once.

Tooka trotted to the top of the hill above his lair.

He took a deep breath, intending to let out a fierce, earsplitting roar.

Then he belched instead.

His stomach still wasn't quite right. Those berries had really done a number on him. It was annoying, but it made him all the more eager to settle his stomach by putting a nice, juicy meal of Floral Essence–flavored flesh in there.

He took another deep breath, then roared so loudly that every bird within five miles suddenly took flight.

🐾 🐾 🐾

Back at the clearing, the Rockball final was about to start when the sound of the tiger's roar reached the humans' ears. Everyone froze.

"TOOKA!" yelled a caveman. In an instant, the entire clan turned and ran for the cave, right past a frightened-looking Marisa.

She looked down at the sharpened stake in her hand, carefully weighing it.

Could they make a tiger trap with just one stake? Was there time to stick it faceup in the bottom of the pit, cover the pit opening with leaves, and create some kind of lure to get the tiger to step over the pit and fall in?

Almost definitely not.

But what choice did they have? This was an emergency.

Marisa looked around for Dug. He was calmly making his way toward the cave. A frightened Tom was right behind him.

"Dug! Make trap! Kill Tooka! Help!" Marisa yelled, pointing first at her stake and then at the pit.

Dug shook his head. Then he pointed to Tom.

"Tom kill Tooka. Do-dee-doot-doot."

Tom froze. "Wait—WHAT?!"

Suddenly, Marisa understood the cavepeople's strange lack of fear about the tiger.

"They think it was your phone!" she told Tom. "They don't realize we poisoned him! They think you used the phone to make the tiger throw up!"

"Oh! No! Nooooo. No-nee-no-no!" Tom grabbed Dug by the arm. "Tom no kill Tooka!"

"Do-dee-doot-doot," Dug insisted. "Do-dee-doot-doot magic rock. Magic rock kill Tooka."

Tom's head wagged in a frantic "no" as he pulled his phone out of his pocket and held it up for Dug to see. "No! Magic rock no more magic! Just rock! See?"

Tom pressed the buttons on the dead phone, then handed it to Dug.

Dug's eyes widened. He poked at the phone's buttons himself.

"Magic rock no magic?" he asked.

"NO!" Tom and Marisa yelled it together. "MAGIC ROCK NO MAGIC!"

Just then, a second and much louder roar reached their ears.

Tooka was getting closer.

Dug looked down at the phone. Then he turned and looked back at the pit, just a few steps behind them.

He scratched his chin thoughtfully.

Then he looked at Marisa. "Tooka. Pit." Beckoning for her to follow, he walked over to the pit.

Marisa couldn't imagine they had enough time to build the trap before the tiger showed up. But they had to try, or somebody was going to get eaten.

She followed the clan leader to the edge of the pit.

"Tooka trap?" she asked him.

"Marsha pit," Dug answered.

Then he threw her into the pit.

Marisa tumbled to the bottom of the ten-foot-deep pit, landing hard on her side. She was too stunned to scream.

Tom wasn't. "AAAAAAAIIIIIEEEEEEEE!" she heard him shriek.

Back at ground level, Tom stared at Dug in horror.

"WHY DID YOU DO THAT?!" he yelled.

"Tom urf Tooka nurf Marsha dadurf," Dug explained.

If Tom could speak caveperson, he would've understood what Dug was saying: *"Tom, your childlike scream of horror makes me think you're probably a little confused about our belief system. So let me explain. I'm going to try to do this quickly, because if we stand out here too much longer, there's a good chance we'll be eaten by a tiger.*

"We are a primitive, frightened, and easily confused people.

When something has great power to hurt us—whether it's a volcano, a bolt of lightning, or a man-eating tiger—it freaks us out. So our standard reaction to that kind of power is to bow down and worship it. We're basically thinking, 'If we pray to you, maybe you won't hurt us.'

"*For a pretty long time now—years, really—we've been worshipping Tooka the tiger. Haven't you seen the drawing on the cave wall, with all of us holding our hands in the air, getting ready to bow down to a giant Tooka?*

"*Frankly, it's been kind of a mixed bag. Worshipping Tooka hasn't exactly stopped him from eating us. But over the years, we've come to an understanding with him that gives us a little bit of control over the process.*

"*The deal we have with Tooka is that when he gets hungry, he roars to give us a heads-up. It's basically a 'Hey, put some food on the table!' roar. We dug this pit, which is too deep for a human to climb out of, but not too deep for a tiger. And when we hear him coming, we throw a tribe member into the pit. Then Tooka comes along, jumps in the pit, eats the person at the bottom of it, then jumps out again and goes about his day.*

"*On the one hand, it's a bad deal for whoever's in the pit. But on the other hand, it's a good deal for the rest of us. Because it lets us—and by 'us,' I mean me, because I'm in charge here—make the decision about who Tooka gets to eat.*

"Usually, I just toss in the most annoying person in the tribe. I think we can all agree that right now, it's Marsha. All that 'don't poop in the cave!' and 'let's do some weird stuff with seeds in the ground!' business didn't exactly make her a lot of friends around here.

"Interestingly enough, up until thirty seconds ago, there's NO WAY I ever would've tossed Marsha in there. Because when you guys first showed up, and you somehow defeated Tooka, and you had a magic rock? Well, this is obviously a little embarrassing now, but the whole thing had me thinking YOU were a god, or at least your rock was. And we should be worshipping you and your rock instead of Tooka.

"Crazy, right? I know. But it seemed to fit the facts. And we were pretty excited about it! I mean, in all the time we've been worshipping Tooka, he never once taught us anything as cool as Rockball. So we were thinking we'd really traded up here.

"But then your magic rock died. So we're back to square one—worshipping Tooka, leaving him human sacrifices, the whole deal.

"Anyway, once Marsha's screams have died out and Tooka's done eating her, I think

128

we'll be able to look back on all this and laugh. In the short term, though, we should get inside the cave. Because what's about to happen in that pit isn't going to be pretty. And if Tooka sees us just standing here yakking, he might eat us, too. He's kind of a jerk that way. Let's go."

Dug turned and headed for the cave entrance. Dumbfounded, Tom stared at him for a moment, then rushed to the edge of the pit.

"Are you okay?" he called down to Marisa.

"No! I'm stuck in a pit! With a tiger coming!"

"Don't worry! I'll get you out of there!"

"How?"

"I have no idea!" Then he thought for a second. "Wait— how about a vine? I can get a vine from a tree and use it to pull you out!"

"Yes! Hurry!"

Tom ran off, past the cave entrance and into the forest.

Marisa barely had a moment to wonder if he'd get back in time. Another roar erupted from the bottom of the clearing, so loud and close it hurt her ears.

Tom wasn't going to get back in time. The tiger was coming for her.

WHOA! I didn't see this plot twist coming! See page 246.

Saber-toothed tigers have an outstanding sense of smell. Even from the far end of the clearing, Tooka's nose told him that Floral Essence was trapped in the pit. Not only that, but a lingering scent of Cool Breeze All Day was wafting over to him from the woods above the cave entrance.

A plan for the day quickly unfolded in Tooka's mind. He'd toy with Floral Essence for a bit, have a little snack—half a leg, maybe, just enough for some quick energy. Then he'd leave her writhing in agony at the bottom of the pit while he hunted Cool Breeze in the forest. He'd enjoy a little cat-and-human game with Cool Breeze, let him think he could actually escape. Then he'd pounce on him from out of nowhere, eat part of an arm, and "accidentally" set him free so Cool Breeze could try to run away again, which was always terribly amusing.

After a few hours, he'd settle down to a full meal of whoever tasted better. Then he'd drag the other one back to his lair for leftovers.

It'd be the perfect combination of food and fun.

Tooka slowly padded across the clearing toward the pit, letting the drool run down his teeth as he savored the thought of what was about to happen.

◉ ◐ ◑

At the bottom of the pit, Marisa was also focused on what was about to happen—and, most importantly, whether there were any versions of what-happens-next that didn't end with her gruesome and bloody death.

She looked around for a way out. There was nothing. Just ten-foot-high dirt walls, a few scattered bones— *human bones? almost definitely*—and the sharpened stake that she'd been holding when Dug pushed her into the pit.

The bones were useless.

The stake, however . . .

◉ ◐ ◑

As Tooka approached, he could hear frantic, breathless digging coming from the bottom of the pit. Floral Essence was clawing at the dirt, desperate to escape.

How tragic! How hilarious! This meant Floral Essence

was going to put up a struggle, which would make for even more fun.

Just before he reached the edge of the pit, the digging stopped. He peered down inside at his prey.

Floral Essence looked up at him with terror in her eyes. She was smack in the middle of the pit, contorted in an odd position. Her legs were bent in a crouch, but her back was so straight it nearly arched.

How strange. Was she injured? Tooka hoped not. He preferred to do the injuring himself.

He uttered a long, low growl. The sound of it made Floral Essence's eyes widen even more. Her whole body was shaking with fear. Good stuff!

Tooka shifted his weight back on his haunches, preparing to pounce.

Not too fast, though—better to let her escape the initial attack. After all, she wasn't going anywhere.

◑ ◑ ◐

Marisa was trying not to tremble, but she couldn't help it. The tiger was staring down at her, saliva dripping from its massive curved teeth. She saw Tooka rear back, getting ready to pounce on her.

Marisa crouched a little lower, tensing her muscles for her own leap.

Tooka pushed off with his back legs and leaped, front paws splaying out in front of him. As he closed the distance between them, he saw Floral Essence leap out of the way, diving toward the far side of the pit.

Perfect! He'd land on all fours, then slowly corner her against the wall.

But wait . . .

Not all of her had leaped out of the way.

She'd left something behind.

Something long and rigid. It was stuck firmly in the ground, just short enough that he hadn't seen it behind her back when he began his jump.

He was going to land directly on top of it, with the full force of his body.

And it looked rather . . . sharp.

Bonk! Marisa had put so much muscle into her leap that she hit her head on the far wall of the pit. As she crumpled to the ground, she heard a noise behind her.

It was like nothing she'd ever heard before. Sudden, loud, and sharp—and yet somehow squishy and wet at the same time. It was sort of a . . .

SQUUUICK!

As his four paws hit the ground—not quite as hard and fast as they should have—Tooka heard the noise, too.

More than that, he *felt* it. It was a horrible feeling—a sudden, burning pain that shot from his belly all the way up through his back.

It felt like someone had just driven a stake through his entire body.

He jerked his head back to turn around, only to discover that he couldn't turn . . . because, much to his surprise, someone HAD just driven a stake through his entire body.

Tooka was pinned like an appetizer on some giant toothpick.

He looked back at Floral Essence, staring wide-eyed at him. She didn't seem terrified anymore. Instead, she looked amazed. Shocked, even.

Not as shocked as he was.

SHE was supposed to be the appetizer! Not him!

In an instant, it had all gone horribly wrong.

This was definitely the worst day of Tooka's life.

It was also the last.

WHOOO!
That was exciting!
See page 250.

21

Her heart hammering against her ribs, Marisa slumped back against the wall of the pit as she watched the life go out of the tiger's eyes.

She'd done it! She'd killed a man-eating tiger!

And now she was stuck inside a pit with a man-eating tiger corpse.

She wasn't sure what to do next. It was a very unusual situation.

Dug stood just inside the cave, staring out at the pit with the rest of his clan. They'd all watched Tooka leap inside, and they were waiting for the screams of agony that always followed.

But this time, there hadn't been any screams. All they'd

heard was a strange noise that sounded like *squuuick.* And then . . . nothing.

Was she too frightened to scream? Had Tooka ripped out her throat? If so, why hadn't they heard the sound of her flesh being torn apart?

Dug tapped his foot impatiently. He wanted to get this over with so they could go back to playing Rockball.

◑ ◐ ◒

Tom sprinted back into the clearing with a long, thick vine coiled in his hands. He expected to find a tiger advancing toward the pit.

But there was no tiger anywhere in sight. Tom ran to the edge of the pit and looked down.

"OHMYGOSH!"

Marisa beamed up at him. "I did it! I killed the tiger! He tried to kill me, but I killed him!"

Tom was amazed. "WOW! You're a rock star!"

"Can you help me out of here?"

"Oh! Right!" Tom tossed down one end of the vine. Marisa grabbed hold, and he hoisted her up out of the pit.

They hugged. Ordinarily, neither of them was the hugging type, but it seemed appropriate.

"How did you do it?" Tom asked.

"I dug the stake into the ground. Then I crouched in

front of it until the tiger started to jump on me. When he did, I leaped out of the way."

"That's amazing! You're like a superhero!"

They heard a voice.

"Tooka?"

It was Dug. He was gingerly walking toward them, keeping a wary eye on the pit. The rest of the clan was a few feet behind him, looking confused and frightened.

"Tooka dead!" Marisa told him, grinning from ear to ear.

Dug reached the edge of the pit and looked down. His eyes widened.

"Marsha . . . kill . . . Tooka?"

Tom and Marisa both nodded happily.

Dug's face darkened. "DUG KILL MARSHA!"

The smiles vanished. Dug started toward Marisa, raising his hands in an "I'm-going-to-strangle-you" gesture.

Shocked, Marisa turned and sprinted for the trees as Tom stepped between her and Dug. "No, Dug! No kill Marsha!"

"Kill Marsha!" Dug repeated, trying to step around Tom.

Tom moved the same way, blocking him. "No! Why?"

"Ooga Tooka booga Marsha!" Dug yelled.

Lacking any formal training in caveperson language,

Tom had no way of knowing what this meant, which was: *"Are you kidding me? Do you know how many years my clan spent worshipping Tooka? We had a real history together! Oh, sure, we had our differences. He ate a lot of us. It wasn't ideal. That's why we were willing to take a chance on worshipping you and your magic rock instead.*

"But you can't go telling us your magic rock is dead and we shouldn't worship you—and then kill our tiger god! Where does that leave us? We've got nobody left to worship! It's anarchy! So you'll excuse me if I feel personally obligated to avenge the death of our tiger god by killing Marsha."

With that, Dug shoved Tom out of the way and started to run after Marisa.

"Dug! Stop!" Tom yelled.

Dug didn't stop. Tom had to think quickly. What could distract Dug from killing Marisa?

"Rockball, Dug! ROCKBALL!"

Dug stopped, pulling up short a few yards from the trees. In his anger, he'd forgotten about the Rockball final. He looked back at his tribe. Then at the forest where Marisa had just disappeared.

Then he nodded. "Rockball."

There would be plenty of time to avenge his tiger god after the game.

Marisa sprinted through the forest, her lungs burning from the effort. The day before, while searching for branches to turn into stakes, she'd passed a cave on a hillside about halfway between the clan's camp and the lake where they'd first landed. The little cave was narrow and deep, making it a perfect hiding place.

Except for the bats.

There were over a hundred of them, asleep in a crevice in the back. When a red-faced, out-of-breath Marisa stumbled into the cave, she woke them up. The bats all took flight in a panic, flitting past her as she ducked and covered her head with her arms.

Oh, great. Bats.

At least they're better than people. Bats won't try to kill me for no reason.

Marisa couldn't understand what had gone wrong. Killing that tiger should've been a triumph. She'd saved the tribe!

But instead of thanking her, Dug had tried to kill her. It made no sense. It was totally unfair.

Marisa started to cry. Once she got started, it was hard to stop. She sobbed until her whole body shook.

She wasn't just crying over Dug wanting to kill her . . . or being all alone in a bat-infested cave . . . or being stuck forever in 10,000 B.C. thanks to a time machine that had completely upstaged her whole life's work.

She was crying over all of it.

All she'd ever done was try to help people. She'd invented a solar panel to try and help mankind solve its energy and environmental problems. It had taken her ten years to do this! She'd showed the cave people how to plant crops so they wouldn't starve. She'd saved them from a man-eating tiger!

And what did she get for it, every single time? Ignored. Or worse. Sometimes much worse.

She cried so hard she almost didn't hear Tom calling her name.

"Marisa?!" Tom yelled as he wandered through the forest. "It's me! Tom! Are you there? Marisa?"

A distant, sorrowful voice finally replied. "Over here."

Tom followed the sound of her voice to the little cave entrance. It took him a moment to realize how upset she was.

"Hi!"

"Hey."

"Are you okay?"

"Not really," Marisa said with a sniffle. She wiped her tears on her dirty sleeve. "Do they still want to kill me?"

"Hard to tell. They're playing Rockball now." Tom sat down next to her. "I'll try to talk to them. It's kinda hard, though. I don't really speak caveman."

Marisa shook her head, defeated. "What's the point?"

"Well, it seems like we need to get along with them. I mean, it's been kind of a while now, and nobody's shown up to rescue us . . . " Tom lowered his voice. "I'm starting to think we might be stuck here."

"I've been telling you that all along! Nobody's coming back for us."

Tom thought for a moment. "Maybe we could build our own time machine."

Marisa was dumbfounded. "Out of what? Rocks and sticks?"

"We'll figure it out! Right now, we're the two smartest scientists in the history of the world!"

Emotionally wrecked as she was, Tom's can-do optimism made Marisa even angrier than usual. "You're not a scientist, Tom," she said in a bitter, seething voice.

"Yeah, I am! Just not officially. I'm like a scientist-to-be. A janitor-slash-scientist."

"No, you're not. You're just a janitor-slash-janitor. That's all you were EVER going to be. They were just using you to clean up their messes."

"Who was?"

"All of them! From Palindrome on down. You were desperate, so they played you for an idiot."

The words hit Tom like a slap in the face. In his head, he quickly replayed his whole history at CEASE, from his job interview to the moment when he lost half a finger wrangling Dr. Palavi's black hole.

Deep down, he knew Marisa was right. And it hurt like nothing he'd ever felt before.

"Why would you say that?" he whispered.

"Because it's true. People are horrible. Join the club."

Tom could feel his own tears starting to well up. "Just

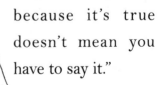 because it's true doesn't mean you have to say it."

When she heard the pain in his voice, Marisa realized how much she'd just hurt him.

"I'm sorry," she said. "I didn't mean—"

"Yes, you did." He stood up. "All I've ever been is nice to you. I don't know why you couldn't be nice to me."

"Tom! Wait!"

But it was too late. He was already gone.

By the time Marisa got up and out of the cave, Tom was twenty yards away, walking back toward the clan.

"Tom! Come back! Please! I'm sorry!"

Tom didn't say a word. He just kept going.

She wanted to follow him. But he was headed back to a group of people who Marisa was pretty sure would kill her on sight.

All she could do was go back into her cave and cry some more, and curse herself for having been mean to the only person who'd showed her kindness in twelve thousand years.

For all the unfair things that had happened to her, this felt even worse.

Because this time, she knew it was her fault.

This is making me SO sad! See page 253.

Meanwhile, twelve thousand years and a few hours later, Dr. Palindrome was working late in Marisa's old lab at CEASE, putting his name on the last of her lab reports. The takeover was complete. As far as anyone could tell, he was now the creator and sole owner of Marisa's solar panel invention. Once he announced it to the world, he'd become instantly famous and only slightly less instantly rich.

Finished, he sat back with a satisfied smile. It had been surprisingly easy to steal the entire life's work of a brilliant but friendless orphan.

There ought to be a law against this, he thought to himself.

Then he thought again.

Actually, I'm sure there IS a law against it. Several,

probably. And I've just broken all of them.

Good thing Dr. Morice was a friendless orphan, or I'd be on thin ice right now.

On his way out of the building, he stopped in the CEASE auditorium, where Dr. Vasquez was also working late. Her time machine was set to be revealed to the world in a press conference the next morning, and she was making some last-minute adjustments.

It had been quite a challenge getting the machine ready in time. Not only did the huge caved-in section and the dozens of little pockmarked dents need hammering out, but the remote control fetcher had mysteriously disappeared. Dr. Vasquez had tried to build a replacement, but the parts for it were so rare and difficult to obtain that it would've delayed the announcement for weeks.

So Dr. Vasquez had decided not to use a fetcher at all for the big announcement. Instead, she was going to demonstrate the time machine by taking herself back in time.

The world's first time traveler!

(Actually, she'd be the third. But nobody in the present knew about Marisa and Tom's one-way trip except Dr. Palindrome. And he was keeping his mouth shut, for obvious reasons.)

"Hello, Doctor!" Despite the late hour, Dr. Vasquez was very chipper.

"Hello to you, Doctor!" Dr. Palindrome was chipper, too. "All set for tomorrow?"

"Just about! I've finished fixing all the damage. Now I just need to pre-program the machine for my maiden voyage."

"Have you decided where you're traveling to yet?"

"It was a tough choice. But after the memorial service, I asked myself, 'If I were Tom Edison, where would I want me to go?' And I figured it out!"

"Not back to 10,000 B.C.?" Dr. Palindrome's heart skipped a beat. If Dr. Vasquez went back in time and stumbled upon Tom and Marisa, it'd ruin his whole plan—and almost certainly send him to jail.

"Oh, heavens, no," Dr. Vasquez chuckled. "It took me days to fix up this machine after the beating it took back in the Stone Age. You won't catch me within a thousand years of THAT era again."

Dr. Palindrome breathed a sigh of relief as Dr. Vasquez continued.

"No, I'm going back to 1879—to the exact date when the REAL Tom Edison invented the lightbulb! Then I'll get him to sign that *Star Trip* poster in honor of our

Tom. I think Tom would really appreciate that."

"Oh, definitely!" said Dr. Palindrome, nodding vigorously. "It's VERY touching. And SO much wiser than traveling back to the Stone Age. The LAST thing our Tom would want is to see you put the 'Tom machine' at risk by going back to such a dreadful era."

"I'm so glad you agree," beamed Dr. Vasquez. "I don't know what was going on back in 10,000 B.C., but it must've been a real nightmare."

"Indeed." Dr. Palindrome headed for the door. "Good night, Dr. Vasquez—can't wait to see you become rich and famous!"

"You, too, Dr. Palindrome. That solar panel idea is aces!"

"It really is, isn't it? I'm SO glad I came up with it. Toodles!"

The sun was setting when a miserable Tom shuffled back into the clan's cave. He'd done a lot of soul-searching since he left Marisa, and it had been very painful. Realizing you've spent your life dreaming an impossible dream . . . while the people you counted on to help make it come true have been feeding you a pack of lies while cruelly taking advantage of you . . .

Well, let's just say it feels pretty lousy.

"Hey, everybody."

The clan members grunted their hellos.

"Rrrr."

"Hrrr."

"Grrr."

Dug was sitting on the ground with half a dozen small rocks spread out in front of him. As the clan's men looked over his shoulder, Dug moved two rocks closer to the center of the spread. He muttered an explanation, and the others nodded.

"Whatcha up to?" Tom asked. "Working on some Rockball strategy?"

Dug looked up at him, confused.

"Rockball? Strategy?"

Tom tried to remember which words Marisa had taught the cavemen.

"Strategy. Uh . . . plan? Rockball plan?"

Dug shook his head. "Not Rockball plan," he said. "Kill Marsha plan."

"Oh, geez," gulped Tom.

🦇 🦇 🦇

"Marisa!" Tom yelled as he ran into her cave.

Marisa winced at the sudden noise. "Watch out for the—"

"AAAH!"

"—bats."

Startled into flight by Tom's yell, a hundred bats flitted out of the cave. Several of them smacked Tom in the face on their way out.

As he flailed his arms and spit bat hairs out of his mouth, Marisa took the opportunity to apologize.

"I'm SO sorry for what I said before. It was mean, and stupid, and—"

"—also true," said Tom. "Those scientists really DID dupe me. But don't worry about that. We gotta get out of here! The cavemen are coming to kill you!"

"What?!"

"We gotta run! Far away! C'mon!"

Marisa followed him out of the cave. They headed across the wooded hillside in the opposite direction of the clan, moving as fast as they could in the dim light of the moon.

"Where are we going?" Marisa asked.

"It doesn't matter! We just gotta get as far away as possible. Then maybe we'll start our own clan. Or find a new one that doesn't have such weird ideas about tigers."

"Do they want to kill you, too?"

"Me? No. We get along fine! I think one of the women wants to set me up with her daughter."

Marisa began to slow down. It was hard to run through a dark forest without tripping on anything. But it was even harder to run with all the guilt that was weighing her down.

"You can't run away with me," she said.

"Why not?"

"You need to stay with the clan. You've got a good situation there. I'm not going to ruin it for you."

"Are you kidding? I wouldn't let you go off alone! We're in this together!"

Hearing Tom's words made Marisa choke up a little. "Wow. You're a really good person."

"So are you," Tom told her.

"I'm not, though," Marisa said. "Or maybe I am, but I just don't know how to show it. I'm TERRIBLE with people. I can't talk to them, I can't relate to them. Half the time, I don't even want to be around them. But you're just the opposite. You're AMAZING with people. They love you!"

Tom was glad it was dark so she couldn't see him blush. "You're amazing, too! Just in a different way. You're the smartest person I've ever met!"

Marisa snorted. "Being smart isn't much good if you can't get along with anybody."

"Are you kidding? I'd MUCH rather have your brains. People skills without smarts aren't that hot, either." He held up his hand. "That's how I lost half this finger to a black hole!"

The forest's trees suddenly gave way to a clearing that allowed them to see for miles. Up ahead in the moonlight were the lake and the cliff where they'd first landed.

Marisa stared at the lake as she thought for a moment.

"No, Tom," she said. "You have to go back. You stay with the clan. I'll be fine on my own."

As she turned to leave him, something in the distance caught her eye.

"You can't just go—" Tom started to protest.

"Wait!" She was squinting in the direction of the lake. "Do you see that?"

"See what?"

"Over there, just off the shore. In the shallow water. Something is glowing."

Tom followed her eyes. "Oh, wow! That's weird. It's like green Day-Glo. I didn't think that existed in 10,000 B.C."

"It doesn't," said Marisa. "We've got to get a better look. Follow me!"

She ran off—not downhill, in the direction of the lake, but uphill, toward the cliff where the time machine had landed.

Tom followed her.

t's the fetcher!" Marisa yelped.

They were standing at the spot on the cliff where the time machine had first landed. A hundred feet below them and twenty feet from shore, Dr. Vasquez's remote control glowed green in the shallow water.

"It must have fallen off the outside of the time machine when the boulder hit it!"

"Are you sure it's the fetcher?" asked Tom. "I don't remember it glowing like that."

"It didn't," said Marisa. "The glow is coming from the radioactive ooze it's leaking."

"Will it still work?"

"Probably. But while it's wet and oozing like that, it's highly radioactive. It could be deadly to anybody who tries to pick it up out of the water."

"Say no more," said Tom. He started to walk off. Marisa grabbed his arm.

"Where are you going?"

"To fetch the fetcher!"

"Tom, if you pull it out of the water with your bare hands, it could kill you!"

"That's what they pay me for! Handling deadly radioactive gadgets is my job!"

"But it's a terrible job! I'm not going to let you risk your life for us!"

"What choice do we have?"

"There's got to be a better way. Let me think about it." Marisa chewed on her lip as she pondered the problem. "If we could just build some kind of a crane . . . and use it to pull the fetcher up out of the water . . . we could press the buttons with a stick and call the time machine back."

"Great! So let's build a crane!"

Marisa shook her head. "We can't do that by ourselves. We'd need giant logs, huge lengths of vine spliced together—it'd take half a dozen men to build something like that."

"We'll get the cavemen to help!"

"But they want to kill me."

"Oh! Right. I forgot we were running for your life just

now. How about you hide, and I'll get them to build the crane?"

"Do you feel like you can handle that yourself? Getting a bunch of cavemen to follow a complicated blueprint that's not even written down, when you don't speak their language?"

Tom thought about it. "I can handle the talking-to-them part. But the knowing-what-to-say part? That'd be tough. I'd need a lot of help with that."

"I agree. For this to work, we need *your* people skills and *my* technical skills. So we've got to somehow convince the cavemen that they not only shouldn't kill me but they should also listen to us."

"How do we do that?"

"I have no idea. Are there any *Star Trip* episodes that might be helpful?"

Tom racked his brain. "Yes! Can you make yourself look like a totally different person? Y'know, like with a cosmeto-transmogrification ray?"

"No, I can't."

"Oh. Well, then I've got nothing."

Marisa was silent for a moment, thinking hard.

"I've got it!" she said.

"What?"

"Bat poop!"

"Of course! Wait—what?"

Minutes later, they were back in Marisa's cave, feeling around in the darkness.

"EEEEEW!" Tom wiped his hand on the cave wall. There's a TON of bat poop back here."

"Perfect!" said Marisa.

"I am definitely not following your train of thought."

"Bat poop is extremely high in nitrates, which are the main ingredient in explosives," Marisa explained. "All we need are bat poop, human urine, dry tinder, some empty coconuts—"

"There's a coconut grove down by the river!"

"—and a little bit of fire. Then we can build bombs."

"If we bomb the cavemen, isn't that going to make it hard for them to help us? On account of their getting bombed and whatnot?"

"We're not going to hurt them. We're just going to amaze and frighten them. If a flashlight and the *Fruit Fight* song were enough to get them to worship you, just think what a few bat poop bombs could do."

Tom's eyes widened as he broke into a smile. "GREAT idea! I'll get the bat poop."

The clan was still asleep around their smoldering fire when Tom tiptoed into the cave at dawn, holding a long stick with leaves tied around one end.

He stuck the leafy end into the fire's embers. It lit up, burning brightly enough to wake Dug and the others.

"Morning, guys!" Tom pulled the small torch from the fire and scampered back outside.

The cavepeople all looked at Dug. He shrugged. Then he stood up, stretching the sleepiness from his body. The other men did the same. They had a big day planned. In the morning, they were going to hunt and kill Marisa. Then they planned to celebrate with an afternoon of Rockball.

They'd figured it would take at least a few hours to track down Marisa, so it was a surprise to hear her voice, yelling from the clearing.

"DO-DEE-DOOT-DOOT!"

Dug and the others looked at each other in surprise.

"DO-DEE-DOOT-DOOT!"

They all grabbed rocks and headed outside.

Marisa and Tom stood in the clearing, facing the cave entrance. Tom held the burning torch. Marisa held what looked like a coconut with a rolled-up leaf sticking out of it.

Dug raised his rock, cocking his hand back to throw it at Marisa. The other cavemen did the same.

As they began to advance, Marisa yelled "DO-DEE-DOOT-DOOT!" again.

Dug snorted. Whatever power that sound once had over him and the others was gone now.

Then he saw Marisa hold out the coconut as Tom lowered the torch to it, igniting the rolled-up leaf.

Dug narrowed his eyes. Setting a coconut on fire seemed odd.

It seemed even more odd for Marisa to throw the burning coconut at them.

But those things weren't nearly as odd as what happened next.

The coconut exploded in midair.

The cavemen shrieked in surprise, freezing in their tracks.

Marisa picked up a second coconut with a leaf sticking out of it. There was a small pile of them at her feet.

As the cavemen stared in awe, Tom lit the leaf-fuse again.

"DO-DEE-DOOT-DOOT!" Marisa yelled, throwing the second coconut at them. It hit the ground, bounced twice, and exploded just inches in front of Dug.

He screamed. Dug had never seen an exploding coconut before, let alone two of them.

Marisa picked up a third coconut.

"DO-DEE-DOOT-DOOT!" she yelled again.

The cavemen all looked to Dug for guidance. Dug looked at Marisa. Then he looked at the coconut. Then he looked at all the other coconuts still at her feet.

He let out a long, defeated sigh. "Arsha barsha Marsha," he said.

And by that, he meant: *"Gentlemen, I don't like saying this any more than you like hearing it. But the evidence is clear.*

"First of all, Marsha's making coconuts explode. Raise your hand if you've seen THAT before. No? Me neither. It's mind-blowing.

"Second, she killed our tiger god.

Which I, for one, did not fully appreciate at the time for the massively impressive power move that it was.

"Third, I still don't get the magic rock thing. But I'm no longer wondering why Tom took his cues from Marsha even when he had the magic rock.

"When you add it all up, I think it's obvious Marsha's a god, and if we don't want to end up like those coconuts, we'd better hit our knees. Are you with me? Good. Because I don't want to do this alone."

Marisa and Tom watched the cavemen fall to the ground, raise their hands in the air, and bow down as they chanted "DO-DEE-DOOT-DOOT MARSHA!"

"Awesome!" yelled Tom. He looked at Marisa. "Right?"

She frowned. "Not quite." Then she cupped her hands around her mouth and yelled "MA-RI-SA! MY . . . NAME . . . IS . . . MARISA!"

The cavemen looked at each other. Then they bowed down again. "DO-DEE-DOOT-DOOT MARISA!"

Marisa smiled. She was getting much better at sticking up for herself. "Okay, let's build a crane."

It was a very impressive crane, especially considering that no one involved in making it had ever built one before, and the only tools they had were trees, rocks, vines, and saber-toothed tiger teeth. From a platform of logs built on the shore of the lake, the crane rose ten feet in the air, then jutted twenty feet out over the water. Its tiger-tooth pincers dangled from the ends of two long vines threaded across the crane's arm like a double fishing line on a pole.

Marisa stood atop the cliff high above the crane, calling out directions to Tom and the cavemen as they maneuvered it into position.

"Farther . . . farther . . . okay, stop! Now left a little . . . too far . . . back to the right . . . STOP! That's perfect!"

The tiger-tooth pincers dangled directly over the submerged fetcher.

"Okay, open the pincers!" On Marisa's command, Tom unspooled the vine that controlled the pincers. The teeth slowly separated.

"Now let the line out!" Tom turned his attention to a second line, giving it some play. The pincers sank into the water.

Tom slowly let out more line until . . .

"I think I felt it hit!" Tom yelled to Marisa. "Can you see it?"

"Yes! You're a little too deep. Pull back on the line a little . . . Perfect! Close the pincers!"

Tom pulled back on the pincer line.

"You got it! Pull up!"

Tom began to reel in the second line. Ever so slowly, the fetcher emerged from the water, held between the pincers at the end of the vine.

"We got it!" yelled Tom.

"Start swinging it over!" yelled Marisa.

Tom called out to Edd and Jim, who were manning the crane's arm. "Turn slow!"

They began to turn the arm, swinging the fetcher toward dry land.

"We're doing it!" yelled Tom. "It's coming over! We're going to—"

The fetcher slipped loose from the pincers and fell in the water.

"Oh, rats," said Tom.

"Don't get discouraged!" yelled Marisa. "Let's just do it again."

They did it again.

And again.

And then four more times.

But finally . . .

"We got it! WE GOT IT! WE GOT IT!" yelled Tom as the fetcher finally reached dry land.

"I'll be right down!" yelled Marisa.

Dug and the other cavemen started toward the strangely glowing fetcher. Its control panel was slick with water, and a thin film of radioactive green goo had seeped from one of its seams.

"No touch!" yelled Tom. "No touch! Stay away!"

The cavemen all looked at Dug. He rolled his eyes and shrugged.

"Smurg," he said.

They all nodded, understanding what he meant, which was: *"Don't ask me, gentlemen.*

I have no idea what that thing is or why we can't touch it. To be completely honest with you, I have no idea how the world works anymore."

A few minutes later, Marisa arrived, out of breath from running down the hill next to the cliff.

By then, Tom had selected the perfect three-foot stick for pressing the big red "RETURN" button on the fetcher.

Marisa pointed to the fetcher and addressed the cavemen. "No touch! Stay away! Danger!"

"Do-dee-doot-doot no touch," the cavemen chanted as they raised their arms in the air and lowered them at Marisa in a gesture of worship.

"I really hope this fetcher works," Marisa told Tom. "Being worshiped isn't as much fun as I thought it'd be. It's actually kind of . . . creepy."

"Creepy do-dee-doot-doot," the cavemen chanted, raising and lowering their arms again.

Tom raised the stick. "Ready?"

"Go for it!"

He reached out with the stick and pressed the fetcher's big red button.

◑ ◔ ◓

Twelve thousand years later, the time machine stood on the CEASE auditorium stage, hidden under a large black velvet sheet that was much fancier than the cotton one Dr. Vasquez had used for the initial Show and Tell.

She'd rented the velvet sheet from a local magician who'd charged her thirty dollars. It seemed like a lot of money for just two hours of a giant black velvet sheet's time, but Dr. Vasquez decided it was worth the extra expense. It looked much more impressive than the plain cotton one. Plus, she was about to become fantastically wealthy, so she could afford to splurge.

She stood backstage with Dr. Palindrome, peeking out at the assembled throng of reporters as the CEASE director reviewed the index cards on which he'd written his introductory speech.

"Should we get started?" Dr. Vasquez asked. This was a very big day for her, and on the outside, she looked as composed and confident as ever. On the inside, though, she was so nervous that she had to keep reminding herself not to bite her stylishly green fingernails.

"Ready when you are!" said Dr. Palindrome.

Just then, they heard a strange *whooosh* sound from the stage, followed by a collective gasp from the audience.

Dr. Vasquez poked her head back out to look at the stage and uttered her own gasp of shock.

The black velvet sheet lay in a heap on the floor.

The time machine had disappeared.

🜚 🜚 🜚

Twelve thousand years earlier, the time machine reappeared . . . on top of Dug's foot.

"OOOOOOW!" he yelled, which was the only word in the caveman language that had the exact same meaning as it did in English.

The other cavemen gasped, fell to their knees, and began to bow to the giant metal box that had mysteriously appeared in front of them.

"Do-dee-doot-doot . . . " they chanted.

Dug did not chant. He also didn't fall to his knees, because there was a time machine on his foot. Instead, he just kept yelling.

"OOOOOOW!"

"Sorry, Dug! We'll get that off your foot in just a skosh!" Tom patted Dug on the shoulder as he ran into the time machine.

Dug did not seem to appreciate Tom's concern.

"OOOOW! OOOOW! OOOOW!" he kept bellowing.

"No touch!" Marisa yelled, pointing to the radioactive fetcher.

"Do-dee-doot-doot no touch," the other cavemen chanted.

"I promise we'll send someone back to clean that up!" Marisa ran into the time machine.

Inside the machine, Marisa found Tom staring, confused, at a framed *Star Trip* poster on the floor. "What's an original one sheet for *Star Trip II: Excelsior's Revenge* doing in here?"

"More important question: How does this control panel work?" Dr. Vasquez hadn't bothered to make it user-friendly for anyone except herself. Other than the part of the display that read "10,000 B.C.," nothing made sense . . . except for the green lever that had started all the trouble in the first place.

"Don't we just pull the lever?" Tom asked.

"Fingers crossed," said Marisa as she pulled the green lever forward.

In an instant, the time machine disappeared from the Stone Age.

Since they were standing inside it, so did Tom and Marisa.

With the weight suddenly gone from his foot, Dug stopped screaming and began to hop around on one leg, muttering caveman curse words.

"Haooga?" asked Edd. In caveman language, that meant, *"Dug, are you okay? That looks like it really smarts.*

Also, what the heck just happened? Where'd that giant magic box come from? More importantly, where did it go? Are we ever going to see Tom and Marsha—I mean Marisa—again? And what's this glowing box, and why aren't we supposed to touch it?"

Dug sat down heavily on the crane platform and began to massage his rapidly swelling foot. The other cavemen watched him nervously, waiting for instructions.

Finally, Dug sighed and said, "Gurg." Which meant: *"Gentlemen, I give up. Let's just get up and walk away—or in my case, hobble away—and pretend none of this ever happened."*

The other cavemen nodded in agreement. It had been a very long week for all of them.

Twelve thousand years later, an auditorium full of reporters was buzzing with confusion about the sudden collapse of whatever was underneath that black velvet sheet on the stage.

Backstage, Dr. Vasquez was panicking.

"It's gone! I have no idea why! Or where! Something's catastrophically wrong! We've got to cancel the press conference!"

Curiously, Dr. Palindrome wasn't panicking. Instead, he was trying to stifle the smile that had been threatening to cross his face ever since he realized what an opportunity this was for him.

"I couldn't agree more about the 'catastrophically wrong' part," he told Dr. Vasquez. "But as for the press conference, if we cancel it now, it'll devastate CEASE's reputation. We'd lose all our credibility with the public. It could ruin us!"

Hearing this—and seeing the strange-looking grimace that she didn't realize was just Dr. Palindrome trying desperately not to smile—made Dr. Vasquez's sense of panic much worse. She began to hyperventilate. "I'm so sorry! I'm so sorry!"

"Not to worry, Doctor—I have a solution!" Dr. Palindrome finally allowed his smile to break out.

Dr. Vasquez looked confused. "You know how to bring my time machine back?"

"Oh, heavens, no. Your time machine's cooked. But I'd be VERY happy to save the day by announcing my solar panel invention instead. Back in a jiff!"

He ran to his office to fetch the panel, beaming with excitement at the thought of becoming rich and famous even sooner than he'd expected.

Dr. Vasquez watched him go, still hyperventilating over the fact that she had no idea where her time machine was.

A few feet away, Jason the janitor leaned on a broom as he yelled after Dr. Palindrome.

"Don't take all day, pal! Ninety minutes, tops, and I'm booting everybody out so I can sweep up. Just so you know."

Approximately a hundred and forty years before that very moment, in a nineteenth-century science lab in Menlo Park, New Jersey, a determined young scientist flipped an electrical switch attached to a small carbon filament and took a step back to watch the results.

As the filament began to glow with brilliant light, Tom Edison—yes, THAT Tom Edison—raised his hands in triumph. He'd just successfully created an electric lightbulb!

Unfortunately, his triumph was cut short when a time machine landed on his foot.

"OOOOOOW!" he yelled.

Inside the machine, Tom Edison—OUR Tom Edison—heard the scream and looked out the window into the pained face of one of his idols.

"SORRY!" he yelled to the man. Then he turned to Marisa. "Why does that keep happening? And where are we?"

Marisa looked at the control panel. "Not sure 'where,' but the 'when' is October 21, 1879."

Tom gasped. "OHMYGOSH THAT'S THOMAS EDISON! I knew he looked familiar!"

"How do you know what Thomas Edison looks like?"

"From my Famous Scientist Trading Card set! He's inventing the lightbulb RIGHT NOW! TODAY! Look out the window—that's it over there! And we just landed on his foot."

"OOOOOOOOOOW!" not-our-Tom-Edison kept yelling.

"We've got to save him!" Our Tom started for the door. Marisa grabbed him by the arm. "Wait! First, let's try this—"

She pulled the green lever all the way back.

In an instant, the time machine disappeared.

Tom Edison stopped screaming and began to hop around his lab on one leg, muttering scientist curse words to himself.

He sat down heavily on a lab stool and began to massage his sore foot.

What the heck just happened? he thought to himself.

What was that giant box that appeared out of nowhere? Who were those people inside it?

How's my lightbulb doing?

He looked across the room. The filament was still glowing. The lightbulb worked! It was ready to announce to the world! He was about to become rich and famous! Nothing could stop him now!

Except possibly a deranged-sounding story about a mysterious giant box with people inside it appearing out of nowhere, landing on his foot, and then vanishing again.

If I tell people about this mysterious vanishing box, I'll sound like a lunatic. That could really muck up my whole lightbulb announcement.

Tom Edison looked around his lab. Nobody had seen the giant vanishing box except him.

Maybe I should just pretend this never happened.

And that's what he did.

As her body was flattened into a sheet one atom thick and twisted around itself half a million times, Marisa prepared herself for the worst. She couldn't understand why they'd wound up in Thomas Edison's research lab in 1879, and she had no idea where the time machine would send them next.

Fortunately, the machine was behaving exactly as Dr. Vasquez had pre-programmed it—to go back to 1879 for Thomas Edison's autograph, then return to the press conference just in time for the triumphant climax of her presentation. It landed back in the CEASE auditorium atop the black velvet cloth, three feet behind Dr. Palindrome, at the very moment that he reached the climax of his replacement presentation.

He held up Marisa's solar panel and crowed, "I'VE

SOLVED MANKIND'S ENERGY NEEDS FOREVER! WITH ZERO HARM TO THE ENVIRONMENT!"

The crowd gasped.

Dr. Palindrome beamed. *That was a heck of a gasp!* he thought. *They must really be impressed! Just look at their jaws dropping!*

It took him a moment to realize the jaw-dropping wasn't entirely about the solar panel. In fact, it was mostly about the giant metal box that had just appeared like a magic trick behind him.

The crowd gasped again when Marisa and Tom stepped out. Marisa had heard the end of Dr. Palindrome's presentation, and she was both confused and angry.

"What are you doing with my solar panel?" she demanded.

The question was followed by a moment of stunned silence.

Then an awful lot of things happened at once.

"*Her* solar panel?" yelled at least three reporters.

"Tom's back!" yelled at least five scientists.

"So is Marisa!" Dr. Vasquez yelled. "And my time machine!"

"It's a *time* machine?" yelled at least seven reporters.

"Dr. Morice! So glad to see you again!" Dr. Palindrome

said, trying to stall for time as his eyes darted from one exit to the next.

"Hey, guys!" Tom waved to the scientists. "We had the craziest week ever!"

"That's right!" Dr. Vasquez replied to the reporters. "I've invented a time machine!"

"Wait a minute!" yelled Dr. Overtree. "That's what's-her-name up there! The solar panel woman who ran off to a Buddhist monastery!"

"And TOM is with her!" yelled Dr. Pulaski.

Fifty-eight scientists and a receptionist ran for the stage to greet Tom, back from the dead.

At the exact same time, 106 reporters ran for the stage to question Dr. Martina Vasquez, inventor of the world's first time machine.

And one sneaky weasel of a lab director tried to run for the door.

"Stop that man!" thundered Marisa. "He just tried to steal my idea!"

Fortunately, it is physically impossible for even a very sneaky weasel to push his way past 165 extremely excited people who are all moving in the opposite direction. Dr. Palindrome found himself stuck onstage, blocked by the crush of scientists trying to quiz Tom and the crush of journalists trying to quiz Dr. Vasquez.

"Where *were* you?" Dr. Overtree asked Tom.

"We were stuck in the Stone Age!" Tom replied. "Dr. Morice and I accidentally went back there on the day Dr. Vasquez unveiled the time machine!"

"BOTH of you?" Dr. Overtree turned to Marisa. "But I thought you ran off to a Buddhist monastery!"

"I've never been to a Buddhist monastery in my life! Who told you that?"

"Dr. Palindrome!"

"It's not true!" Tom yelled. "She was with me! We accidentally traveled back in the time machine, and—"

"But that's impossible!" Dr. Salaam interrupted. "We checked the security camera footage! The time machine never left!"

"WHO checked the footage?"

"Dr. Palindrome!" the scientists all answered at once.

"The same guy who just tried to steal my solar panel idea?!" Marisa cried out. "And lied about me being in a Buddhist monastery?!"

"Hey, Dr. Palindrome!" bellowed Dr. Overtree, swiveling his head as he searched the crowd for the director. "Did you know where they were all along? Did you set them up so you could steal the solar panel idea?"

"Where is Dr. Palindrome?"

"Block the exits, everybody!"

Catching a whiff of scandal, some of the reporters who were crowding around Dr. Vasquez for news of the time machine turned around and started asking questions about Dr. Palindrome and the solar panels.

"Is this a scandal?"

"Is the director of CEASE a crook?"

"Where is he?"

"Did anybody block the exits?"

Dr. Palindrome hadn't managed to get to an exit. Instead, he'd ducked inside the only hiding place he could find in the middle of the mobbed stage: the time machine.

And as he listened to the growing anger of the crowd outside, he knew his goose was cooked. It was only a matter of time before he'd wind up in jail.

Dr. Palindrome did not want to go to jail.

There was only one alternative. He pulled on the long green lever.

The time machine disappeared.

WOW!
That was
some climax!!
See page 256.

A hundred and sixty-seven people gasped in surprise.

"Oh, for crying out loud!" moaned Dr. Vasquez. "Not again!"

"Fifty-four more minutes!" yelled Jason the janitor as he tapped his watch. "Then I'm booting you all out so I can clean this place. Just FYI."

After Dr. Palindrome disappeared, there was a lot of yelling, mostly from the reporters. When Dr. Vasquez left the room to go call the police and report a missing time machine, the reporters turned their attention to Marisa.

As she stood on the stage—happy, angry, confused, excited, exhausted, and nervous all at the same time—they yelled question after question at her.

"What was it like being stuck in 10,000 B.C.?"

"Um . . . scary?"

"Are you going to press charges against Dr. Palindrome?"

"Uh . . . probably?"

"How did you come up with your amazing solar panel invention?"

"I, um . . . worked really hard. For a long time."

"Will you be starting a revolutionary new solar panel company?"

"I guess so."

"When?"

"Soon? Maybe?"

As she struggled to come up with answers to all their questions, two thoughts ran through Marisa's head.

The first one was, *This is the kind of attention I always dreamed of getting.*

The second one was, *I don't like this very much.*

"How did you and the janitor end up in the time machine?"

"Excuse me." Instead of answering, Marisa ran off stage and disappeared out the side door.

"Hey!"

"Where's she going?"

"She can't just leave like that! We're having a press conference!"

"Let's go after her!"

"WAIT!" Tom threw himself between the journalists and the doorway. "I'm sure Dr. Morice will be back really soon! In the meantime, I guess I could take your questions."

"I got a question for you!" It was Jason. He loomed over Tom menacingly. "You're the janitor everybody thought was dead, right?"

"That's right!" Tom gave Jason a big smile. In return, Jason gave him an equally big angry glare.

"You know you can't have your old job back just 'cause you're not dead, right? 'Cause that position's been filled . . . by THIS GUY." Jason put up both fists, thumbs sticking out, and pointed at himself. Then he retracted the thumbs, leaving just the fists up as a none-too-subtle warning.

"That's great!" Tom grinned from ear to ear. "Congrats on the new job!"

"Uh . . . thanks." As he shook Tom's outstretched hand, Jason looked confused. He hadn't expected Tom to be so happy about losing his job.

"By the way," Tom said, "there's a missing part from Dr. Vasquez's time machine stuck back in 10,000 B.C. It's leaking deadly radioactive goo, so someone needs to clean it up. Since you're the new janitor, can you handle that? Thanks!"

"What? Huh?"

"Any other questions?" Tom asked the reporters.

They all started yelling at once.

"How'd you get stuck in the time machine?"

"How'd you get back here?"

"What's the deal with your eyebrows?"

◐ ◑ ◓

Marisa darted into her tiny, windowless lab in the darkest corner of the deepest basement at CEASE. Closing the door behind her, she let out a deep sigh of relief. Having to deal with all those reporters and their questions had felt almost as stressful and exhausting as her battle to the death with a saber-toothed tiger.

She walked over to the lab table and took a seat in the same chair where she'd spent most of the past ten years.

Everything was exactly as she'd left it.

Except that Dr. Palindrome had written his name on all of her papers.

She'd have to fix that. But it could wait.

She let out another sigh. Sitting alone in her lab again, after everything she'd been through, was giving her very mixed feelings.

On the one hand, she'd been terribly lonely during all those years in this tiny, windowless room.

On the other hand, it was where she had done the most important work of her life. As hard and frustrating as that work had been, it was also deeply satisfying. She'd created something new. And not just new, but important!

Those solar panels were going to improve the lives of millions.

Being around those groups of people—not just at the press conference, but back with the tribe in the Stone Age—had been hard and frustrating, too.

But unlike inventing the solar panel, it hadn't been satisfying at all.

She just wasn't cut out for that kind of thing.

Maybe being alone was better after all?

No. That wasn't quite it. She wanted to be around people.

Just not very many of them. And not for too long at a stretch.

There was a knock at the door.

"Who is it?"

Tom poked his head in.

"Hey! Sorry to bother you! Are you okay?"

"Yeah. I just . . . needed some alone time."

"I'm sorry! I'll leave." He started to close the door.

"No! It's fine. How was the press conference?"

"It was great! The police came!"

"Really?"

"Yeah! It was really exciting! They're putting a warrant out for Dr. Palindrome! But they were, like, 'We can't travel through time to catch him.' Because I guess they don't have the budget for that or something? So Dr. Vasquez is going to build a second time machine, and then SHE'S going to go back and catch him herself. Oh! Also, she wanted me to ask you if you're available for lunch one of these days. She was going to ask you herself, but you disappeared before she could."

Marisa blushed at the offer. "Okay, definitely yes to lunch. But isn't chasing Dr. Palindrome through time going to be dangerous?"

"Totally! Right? 'Desperate men do desperate things.' That's what Captain Dirk said on *Star Trip* once."

"And how will she know where to look? I mean, couldn't he have gone anywhere?"

"Yeah. But she said the fetcher's designed to track the machine's location. So if she goes back to 10,000 B.C. and gets the fetcher, it'll tell her where Dr. Palindrome is!"

"Did you tell her it's leaking deadly radioactive goo? And we've got to clean it up right away?"

"She knows! The new janitor is going to go with her and take care of that. But he says he has to get paid triple overtime to do it."

"They hired a new janitor?"

"Yeah. I guess they fired me because I was dead?"

Marisa cringed. "Tom, I'm so sorry! I cost you your job!"

"It's fine! It's better this way! You were right—they were kinda just using me. After the press conference, I tried to warn the new guy about that, but he didn't really want to hear it. He's got kind of an attitude."

"You really don't mind losing your job?"

"No! I'm totally cool with it. Hey, are you hungry?"

Marisa suddenly realized that she hadn't eaten in ages. (Literally.)

"Ohmygosh, yes. I'm *starving*."

"Do you want to go grab some lunch in the cafeteria?"

Marisa smiled at the thought.

"I would love that."

◑ ◒ ◓

"Oh, wow, this is delicious," Tom said through a mouthful of sandwich. "The bacon and avocado really take it to the next level."

"The sandwiches are the best thing about CEASE," Marisa replied through her own mouthful. "I'm really going to miss them."

"Wait—you're leaving CEASE, too? Why?"

"Because I need to start a revolutionary new solar panel company."

"Oooooh! Right!"

"I mean, that's kind of the obvious next step, isn't it?"

"Absolutely!" Tom nodded enthusiastically. "You pretty much have to!" His eyes widened. "Oh, geez! I almost forgot—" He pulled a piece of paper from his pocket. "I wrote down all the questions the reporters had for you. Plus their email addresses. So you can just write out your answers and send them back. It seemed like talking to them was really stressing you out. So I figured this might be easier for you."

"Thank you so much!"

"It's my pleasure! I'm really happy for you! This solar panel thing is exciting!"

Marisa looked down at Tom's page of questions. It was neatly written, well-organized, and contained less than ten major spelling errors.

She sat quietly for a moment, thinking to herself.

"So . . . you're unemployed now, right?"

"Pretty much," said Tom.

"Do you know what you'll do next?"

"I dunno. I mean, I LOVE science. But it's like you said

the other day: I'm not really much a scientist." Tom's face fell as he said it. Admitting the truth out loud didn't make it any less painful.

Marisa winced in sympathy. But then the corners of her mouth turned up in a hopeful smile.

"What if you helped run a science-based company? Like, what if you were the public face who took care of all the non-science, working-with-other-people stuff for some other scientist? So they could just focus on their inventions?"

"That would be amazing! But how would I ever get a job like that?"

"I know a revolutionary new solar panel company that'd love to hire you."

Tom leaped up from his seat, grabbing his head with his hands like he was trying to stop the top of his skull from blowing off. "OHMYGOSH, ARE YOU SERIOUS? THAT WOULD BE AMAZING!"

Marisa stuck out her hand with a grin. "Welcome aboard, Employee Number One."

As they shook hands, a voice bellowed from the other end of the room.

"WRAP IT UP, PEOPLE! CAFETERIA'S CLOSED!"

Jason pushed the floor buffer toward them with one

hand while making a "take a hike" gesture with his other.

"Make like a tree and leave! Especially you, Mister I-Don't-Work-Here-Anymore."

"He's my guest," Marisa informed the janitor. "And the cafeteria's open for another hour."

"Not today," said Jason. "I gotta finish buffing by four so I can get in the emergency time machine Dr. Vasquez is speed-building in her lab to send us back in time to clean up her radioactive doohickey. Then we gotta find that Palindrome deadbeat and drag him back here to face arrest. And I gotta get it all done by six so I can get outta here in time to watch round one of the Rockball Cup."

Marisa's and Tom's jaws slowly dropped. *What did he say?*

"The what?" asked Tom.

"Did you say 'Rockball'?" asked Marisa.

"'Course I did! Whaddaya lookin' at me like that for? Like you never even heard of the Rockball Cup? The world's biggest sporting event? That mankind's been playin' for thousands of years? What are you, stupid?"

Tom and Marisa looked at each other. "That is super weird," Tom whispered.

"It sure is," agreed Marisa.

"Should we say anything?"

"No. Let's just go start our company. But maybe we can knock off early, eat some nachos, and watch a little Rockball."

"Great idea!" As they gathered their sandwich wrappers and started for the door, Tom grinned at Marisa. "I'm really looking forward to this whole starting-a-revolutionary-new-company-to-help-mankind thing."

Marisa grinned back at him. "Me, too, partner."

With that, they walked out of the cafeteria, ready to change the world together.

Now, THAT was a satisfying ending! See page 260.

STORY
CREATION
ZONE

TABLE OF CONTENTS

STORY CREATION ZONE

THE MIDDLE

THE END

STORY CREATION ZONE

What's a Story, Anyway?

A story is just a bunch of stuff that happens.

But if you put that stuff together in the right way, it can make you laugh until your sides hurt, cry a river of tears, or turn red with anger. A story can scare the heck out of you. It can make your heart race with excitement or break with sadness.

The right story can even change your life.

Or it can just make you fall asleep, if it's really boring.

Knowing how to tell a good (and non-boring!) story is a pretty cool thing. That's the purpose of the Story Creation Zone: to help you tell good stories of your own.

There are gazillions of different kinds of stories. They range from a ten-second one you tell your friends about a weird thing that happened on the way to school, to a seven-book series about an epic battle between wizards for the future of the planet.

There are short stories, long stories, funny stories, sad stories, exciting stories, true stories, totally made-up stories, partly-true-and-partly-made-up-stories . . . the list is endless.

But every single story ever told has one thing in common:

A story is about a **character** with a **problem**.

That's ALL a story is. The character can be anyone or anything—it doesn't even have to be a person. It can be an animal, a monster, a tree, a toy that comes to life, or whatever you want. Some stories have dozens, even hundreds of characters, but every story has at least one.

The problem can also be anything at all. It can be huge and earthshaking, like saving the world from an evil mastermind! Or getting stuck in the Stone Age and having to figure out how to get back to the present day! Or it can be smaller and more personal, like getting in an argument with a friend and trying to figure out how to make peace with them even though you're still mad.

A good story has three parts: a beginning, a middle, and an end.

In the **beginning** of the story, we meet the character and find out what the problem is.

In the **middle** of the story, the character tries to solve the problem.

At the **end** of the story, the character either solves the problem or fails to solve it.

That's it! That's ALL you need. In the pages that follow, we're going to give you a lot of info about storytelling. If you ever get stuck, flip back to this page and remember the basics: All you need is a character with a problem. Everything else is just details.

Want to get started writing your own story? Grab a pencil and paper and keep reading!

How Does the Story Creation Zone Work?

In the Story Creation Zone, we'll explain the basics of storytelling and give you tips for making your writing soar. We'll also suggest some simple activities you can use to create *any* kind of story, about *any* character or problem you can imagine, at *any* length. By the time we're done, you'll have an amazing story of your own!

As you read through, you'll see four kinds of entries:

Storytelling 101: These are the essential parts of any story. If you imagine your story as a house, then Storytelling 101 will show you how to lay the foundation, put up the walls, and add a roof. Without these, your house will collapse!

Write Like a Pro: These are useful tips to make your writing and storytelling more interesting and colorful. If your story is a house, these are the tools for helping you paint, decorate, and furnish it so it looks awesome.

🧪 **Science Fiction Zone**: *Stuck in the Stone Age* is a type of story called science fiction, or sci-fi. Sci-fi stories are full of wild and strange ideas, which we'll talk about in these entries. If sci-fi is the kind of story house you want to build, look here for ideas!

🌩️ **Idea Storm**: Here's where you build a house of your own! These are simple, fun activities to help you create your own story. If you do them all, you'll have everything you need for an awesome story.

As you think about creating your story, keep in mind two important things.

First, **your story is not going to start out perfect!** You're going to make mistakes, change your mind, cross things out, get stumped, and just generally make a mess, both in your head and on the page.

AND THAT'S GREAT! That's how creativity and writing work! They're MESSY. **All writers make tons of mistakes**. The best stories come from RE-writing your original ideas. Geoff Rodkey, the author who built *Stuck in the Stone Age* out of Vince's idea, had a bunch of ideas that didn't work out. He wrote whole chapters of the book that he wound up deleting! He also added a bunch of new ideas later.

As you write your story, give yourself the space to change your mind and rework things. If you're writing with a pencil and paper, it can help to skip lines so there's room on the page to cross things out and rewrite them. You can always clean things up in your next draft.

For example, here's how that paragraph looked in our FIRST draft:

> ~~So~~ as you write your story, give yourself the space to change your mind and ~~decide if you hate everything~~ rework things ~~about your story.~~ If you're writing in pencil and paper ~~if you should ALWAYS ALWAYS~~ it can help to skip lines so there is room on the page to ~~erase so hard you tear a hole in the paper.~~ cross things out and rewrite them. You can always ~~throw the whole thing out and start over.~~ clean things up in your next draft.

Second, give yourself PERMISSION TO GET WEIRD. Some of the best ideas sound incredibly weird ... at first. In order to come up with an amazing story, you need to try out lots of ideas on the page to see how they look. Let your imagination run wild! Get that weird idea down on paper in a first draft! Once you do, you might decide it's the best idea ever! Or you might decide you don't like it at all. If so, that's fine! Just cross it out and write something else! That's why pencils have erasers and computers have delete keys—don't be afraid to use them!

 Hey, readers, see that ? Every time it shows up, that means it's the end of the section. If you got here by flipping forward from page 2 when we told you to, flip back to page 2 now!

Seriously, flip back. Get out of here!

 Or don't. That's fine, too. Hey, we're not your parents. We're not going to tell you how to live your life.

THE BEGINNING

🏗️ Storytelling 101: What Kind of Story Is This?

One way to start writing a story is by asking yourself what *kind* of story you want to write. Most stories fall into categories called **genres**. *Genre* is the type of story you're telling—for example, drama, comedy, science fiction, mystery, romance, horror, or historical fiction.

It's helpful to know your story's genre for two reasons.

First, it helps set the **tone** of your story. Do you want to write something that makes your audience laugh, like in a comedy? Do you want to scare their pants off, like in a horror story? Depending on the answer, you'll probably tell your story in very different ways.

For example, *Stuck in the Stone Age* is a comedy—so when Hank the janitor turns into a chameleon, it happens in a (hopefully) funny way. If *Stone Age* were a horror story, Hank might have eaten Dr. Palindrome instead of just yelling at him, and the audience might have been more frightened than amused.

Second, knowing your genre can help you come up with ideas for your story. In addition to being a comedy, *Stuck in the Stone Age* is a science fiction story. It's fun to write science fiction because science itself is crazy—it's full of wild, strange, and amazing but true things that happen in real life. Sci-fi is different from fantasy, because the things that happen in science fiction are usually not magic. They're things that could *maybe* actually happen one day.

You probably know some science fiction stories. They can involve:

- Spaceships flying to faraway planets
- Superintelligent computers or robots
- Getting a glimpse of the distant future, where amazing technology is everywhere
- Scientists creating crazy inventions (like time machines)

Before people ever traveled in space, science fiction writers were imagining what it might be like. Before there were internet-connected computers in our homes, sci-fi writers were imagining devices just like that. Science fiction lets us imagine a world we'd like to live in someday (or a world we'd never, ever want to live in!).

203

Write Like a Pro: Starting Stories Off with a BANG!

Have you ever picked up a book, read a page, and then put it down because you're just not into it?

And have you ever picked up a book, read the first page, and thought, "OHMYGOSH, WHAT'S GONNA HAPPEN NEXT??"

THAT'S what you want your reader thinking when they start your story—you want to get them so interested in "What happens next??" that they have to keep going to find out. Sometimes, this is called a **hook**—as in, getting your reader hooked on the story right away.

So how do you write a great opening hook? A bunch of different ways. With action! Or conflict! Or even a startling noise! For example, you could start your story with . . .

KAZOOM!

Your reader will wonder, "What on earth made that 'kazoom!' noise? Was it a spaceship taking off? A robot running at the speed of sound? An exploding volcano?"

It can be anything. Just make sure it's somehow important to your story.

For example, *Stuck in the Stone Age* begins with Hank the janitor yelling: "THIS IS THE LAST STRAW!"

What's the last straw? We don't know! We just know Hank is very angry, and if we want to find out why, we'll have to keep reading.

Remember how we said it's okay to get messy and go back and change things when you write? Here's a secret: A LOT of things got crossed out in the writing of *Stuck in the Stone Age*—and the opening hook was one of them! Geoff Rodkey added Hank's big entrance after he'd written most of the novel. And to make room for it, he threw out the whole first chapter from his early draft. If you aren't in love with the hook you have now, remember you can always go back and improve it later! An artist's work is never finished.

Storytelling 101: The Main Character

Every story has a **main character**. Sometimes, this character is called the hero. You can also use the term *protagonist*, which is a fancy word for "main character." The main character doesn't have to be a person—it could be an animal, an alien, a monster, or even a pencil, as long as the pencil can talk or think.

In *Stuck in the Stone Age,* the main character is Tom Edison. (This name is sort of a joke. As you probably know, there really was a famous scientist named Thomas Edison. He invented the lightbulb, among other things. But our Tom Edison turns out to be much different.)

The main character is usually the person (or animal or pencil) who your audience will root for. When the character faces a **problem**—which will happen, because stories are all about characters facing problems—the reader wants to see the character solve it and succeed. That's why it's important to make the main character as detailed and interesting as possible. Your reader will be spending a lot of time with them and will get to know (and hopefully like) them.

When you're creating a main character, it's helpful to write down the most important things about that character so you can see them all in one place. At the Story Pirates, we like to use a "Character Creator" for this. Here's what our Character Creator looks like for Tom:

☠ CHARACTER CREATOR ☠

CHARACTER'S NAME
Tom Edison (not the famous scientist)

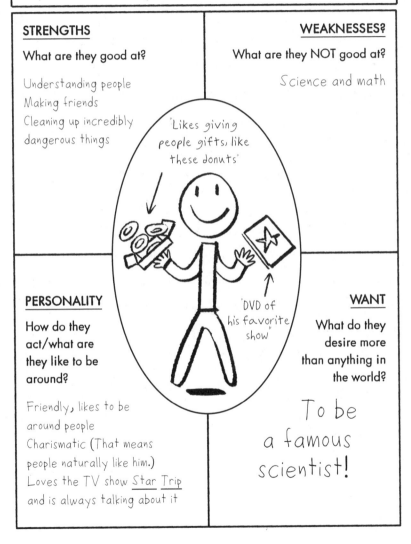

STRENGTHS

What are they good at?

Understanding people
Making friends
Cleaning up incredibly
dangerous things

WEAKNESSES?

What are they NOT good at?

Science and math

"Likes giving people gifts, like these donuts"

"DVD of his favorite show"

PERSONALITY

How do they act/what are they like to be around?

Friendly, likes to be around people
Charismatic (That means people naturally like him.)
Loves the TV show <u>Star Trip</u> and is always talking about it

WANT

What do they desire more than anything in the world?

To be a famous scientist!

Pay special attention to that last box: **what the main character wants**. This is VERY important. Sometimes, the whole story is about the main character trying to get what they want. In this story, Tom wants to be a famous scientist. Trying to achieve that goal is a big part of the story—but it's not the whole story. There's a much bigger problem he'll need to deal with very soon. (Stay tuned!)

Here's one more important tip: The character will be more interesting to read about if you make it *very, very hard* for them to get what they want. One good way to do this is by picking the right **weaknesses**. For example, Tom's weaknesses are that he's bad at science and math. But he's not just bad—he's *so* bad that his physics teacher had to create a new grade for his work (an H, two letters below an F). Plus, he's obsessed with a science fiction TV show called *Star Trip* and thinks all the imaginary things on the show could be real (like something called a "fluotanium capacitor ray"). It's going to be very hard for Tom to get what he wants with these weaknesses—but very interesting for the reader to watch him try.

Science Fiction Zone: Astronauts, Aliens, and So Much More!

How do you create a main character that's right for a science fiction story?

The short answer is: *Any* kind of character can be in a science fiction story. You just need to figure out a reason why the character would be around some weird science experiment, invention, or problem that could *maybe* really happen someday.

Here are a few examples of common science fiction characters:

- Someone flying in an intergalactic spaceship
- An alien
- A regular person in the future with crazy technology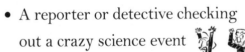
- A reporter or detective checking out a crazy science event
- A scientist
- An adorable kitten with genius-level intelligence

You get the idea. It can be any kind of character, as long as there's going to be some wild and weird science in their future.

🧠 Idea Storm: Main Character

Now you try it! Make up a main character, and use the Character Creator as a guide. It can be any kind of character you want—a human, an animal, or something imaginary. Remember to think carefully about these questions:

- What does my character want more than anything in the world?
- Does my character have any weaknesses that might make getting that thing very, very hard?
- Does my character have strengths that might help them succeed?

While you're brainstorming, don't forget to give yourself PERMISSION TO GET WEIRD. Write down any ideas you want, no matter how weird! You can always change them later.

✏️ Write Like a Pro: Show, Don't Tell

You may have heard at some point that good writers should "**show, not tell**." How do you do that, exactly?

There are a lot of different ways, and we'll discuss a few of them in this book. Here's one big thing to focus on: **Show** the reader what your characters are *doing*, instead of just **telling** facts about what they're like. For example, back in the Character Creator, we said that Tom Edison is friendly and that people naturally like him. But in *Stuck in the Stone Age*, the text doesn't say, "Tom was a friendly character." Instead, it shows what Tom *does* that makes him friendly:

Tom had brought Doris a jelly doughnut (her favorite), which was almost knocked out of his hand by the angry man who stormed out of CEASE just as Tom was walking in.

"Excuse me! Sorry! Have a great day!" Tom said with a smile.

With your own characters, find ways to do the same thing. Don't just take the words out of your Character Creator and tell your reader what the character is like. If your character is friendly (or annoying or sad or hilarious), show this to the reader by writing what the character *does* that's friendly (or annoying or sad or hilarious).

🏗️ Storytelling 101: Villains, Shape-shifters, and Minor Characters

What's the deal with this Dr. Palindrome guy?

Most stories have more characters than just the main

one. Some have hundreds! Every character has a purpose. Take Hank the janitor, for example. He's a **minor character**—he's mostly there to quit his job (so Tom can get hired as CEASE's janitor) and to help show us that the job Tom is taking is very dangerous.

What about Dr. Palindrome? From Tom's point of view, he seems like an **ally**—a "good guy" character who's on Tom's side and might end up helping him solve his problem or get what he wants. He just gave Tom a janitor job and promised it could lead to his dream job as a scientist!

But we know more than Tom—enough to be very suspicious. In Chapter 1, we saw that Dr. Palindrome knows being a CEASE janitor is dangerous, even life-threatening. He doesn't care—he just wants to fill the job. When he tells Tom that taking this horrible job might lead to the scientist job Tom really wants, we're pretty sure Dr. Palindrome is lying.

This makes Dr. Palindrome a likely **villain**. A villain tries to stop the main character from solving the problem—or, in some cases, they're the one causing the problem in the first place. Just like the fancy word for main character is protagonist, the fancy word for "villain" is *antagonist*.

It's often the villain who really makes a story fun and exciting. Think about your favorite books, movies, and TV shows. Is there a villain in them? Now imagine taking that villain out of the story. Would the story be as much fun? Probably not.

Like the main character, a villain can be anyone. If a puppy dog is trying to stop your main character from getting what they want, that puppy can be the villain of your story. If a talking pancake keeps spoiling your character's plans, that talking pancake is a villain. Villains don't ALL have to be evil geniuses or wicked queens or super mutants.

Sometimes, they don't even seem like villains at first. A character who seems good but turns out to be bad, or seems bad but turns out to be good, is a **shape-shifter**. Characters who surprise you like that can be the most fun characters of all, both as an audience and a writer.

So is Dr. Palindrome a villain? Will he end up doing something much worse to Tom? Or will he surprise us and turn out to have a heart of gold? Keep your eye on him as the story continues.

Storytelling 101: ANOTHER Main Character?!

Most stories have just one **main character**. But *Stuck in the Stone Age* has TWO! Dr. Marisa Morice is also a main character. Does that make the story twice as much fun? We think so!

When a story like *Stone Age* has two main characters, they're usually very different. How different are Tom and Marisa? Turn the page to see a Character Creator for Dr. Marisa Morice.

Marisa has a big—and kind of heartbreaking—**want**: She doesn't want to be lonely anymore. This will probably be very hard for her to accomplish, because one of her **weaknesses** is that she gets nervous around other people, so she's not good at making friends. In this chapter, just talking to Tom was stressful for her.

Tom, on the other hand, is great at making friends! It's his biggest **strength**! So what Marisa wants is something Tom already has, and her big weakness is his big strength.

Likewise, Tom wants more than anything to be a scientist—and Marisa's already a brilliant one! Her knowledge of science is her biggest strength, while Tom's lack of science skills is his biggest weakness.

So Marisa's and Tom's wants, strengths, and weaknesses are all **opposites**.

What does this mean for our story? If they can figure out a way to work together, Tom and Marisa might make a pretty great team!

BUT . . . until they do that, they're going to really get on each other's nerves. This conflict is clear in the first words they say to each other, when Tom is excited to meet Marisa, but she's frightened and annoyed by him:

"OHMYGOSH! Aren't you Marisa Morice? The youngest winner in the history of the National Junior Science Competition? HOLY COW! You were Rookie of the Year in my Famous Scientist Trading Card set!"

"Who are you, and why don't you have any eyebrows?"

It's no fun to be annoyed by someone in real life, but reading about someone who's annoyed can be awesome. *Stuck in the Stone Age* is a comedy, and a lot of the humor comes from the fact that the characters are constantly butting heads. Will they ever get along? Can they help each other overcome their weaknesses and get what they want or solve their problem? It will be fun to see what happens, no matter what.

If you decide to put two main characters in your story, you'll need to spend as much time thinking (and writing)

☠ CHARACTER CREATOR ☠

CHARACTER'S NAME

Dr. Marisa Morice-chemical reaction scientist

STRENGTHS

What are they good at?

Science! Math!
She won a science
competition when she
was a kid and has
been working on
science ever
since.

"The smile she gets
when a new invention
is going well"

WEAKNESSES?

What are they NOT good at?

Very nervous around people
Not good at making
friends_even the
other scientists
in the lab where
she works can't
remember her
name.

National Junior
Science
Competition
WINNER

"Award she
won when
she was 11
years old"

PERSONALITY

How do they act/what are they like to be around?

Hard working
Introverted (That means
she likes spending time
by herself.)
Gets embarrassed easily

WANT

What do they desire more than anything in the world?

To not be lonely
(She would like it if
someone would want to
have lunch with her.)

216

about the second one's wants, strengths, and weaknesses as you did for the first one. And to make the story extra interesting, try to make those things the opposite of what they were for your first character.

Storytelling 101: The Setting

The **setting** is where (and when) your story takes place. A setting can be anywhere, from a regular town to an imaginary world. A story can have just one setting or dozens, depending on what happens and where the characters go.

In *Stuck in the Stone Age*, there are two main settings: the CEASE science lab, and the Stone Age of 12,000 years ago.

When you're building a story, it's helpful (and fun!) to imagine tons of details you might find in the setting. What kind of people (or animals or aliens) are around? What are they doing? What's the weather like? Is there scenery? Is it pretty? Ugly? Clean? Dirty? Smelly? Fun? Boring? Is there anything unusual, dangerous, or interesting going on? What's your main character doing there? Do they like it? Do they hate it?

The more you know about your setting, the richer your

story will be. Thinking in detail about the setting can also help you come up with ideas for what should happen in the story.

One good way to help build your setting and keep track of what's going on in it is to draw a map or a picture. For example, here's a map we drew of CEASE:

A drawing like this can also help you keep track of **minor characters** (like Doris the receptionist or the

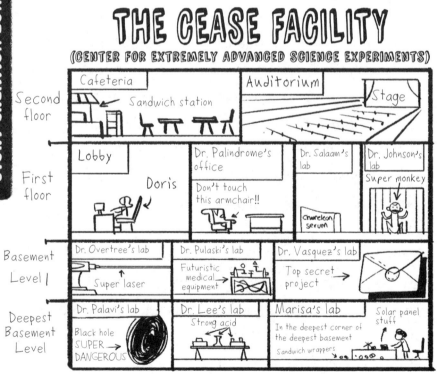

THE CEASE FACILITY
(CENTER FOR EXTREMELY ADVANCED SCIENCE EXPERIMENTS)

other scientists), as well as planning out interesting details for your readers to enjoy (like lasers that go *bew* or supermonkeys that *screech!*).

 ## Science Fiction Zone: Sci-Fi Settings

If you're writing a science fiction story, picking a setting is part of the fun. Will you write about a normal-seeming neighborhood, where a scientific experiment is about to go horribly wrong? Or maybe a place full of futuristic inventions, where wild and amazing things happen every day?

A science laboratory like the CEASE facility is a common science fiction setting. Here are a few others:

- A spaceship
- An ordinary house or city, but in the future
- Another planet
- A secret fortress with advanced technology
- Another dimension: a place that looks like Earth, but has some weird differences (These could be big differences, like dinosaurs never died out so highly evolved velociraptors have built huge cities; or small differences, like toasters were never invented so people make toast by roasting bread over a fire.)

If you're writing a story about time travel, the options are endless: You could set your story in the distant past, the distant future, or anywhere in between! Here are just a few of the many, many options

- Prehistoric times!
- Ancient civilizations like Rome, Egypt, or China
- The Middle Ages
- Big moments in the twentieth century: World War I and II, the moon landing, the sinking of the *Titanic*, and more
- The future: What will life be like in ten years? One hundred years? Ten thousand years? How will people be different, and how will they stay the same? What kind of inventions do they have, and what kind of vehicles do they use? The answers are up to you!

Idea Storm: Settings

Now you try it! Plan out a setting for your story by drawing a map or picture and labeling all the important details.

While you're brainstorming, don't forget to give yourself PERMISSION TO GET WEIRD! Draw as many maps or pictures as you want, and don't worry about whether everything you draw will end up in your story. The more details you can imagine about your setting, the more it'll come to life in your mind.

🏗️ Storytelling 101: Reversals of Fortune

Oh, no! Marisa's plan to get everyone's attention with her invention was going great. BUT THEN Dr. Vasquez totally overshadowed her with the time machine!

This is a great example of one of the basic building blocks of any story: the **reversal of fortune**. A reversal is a change that flips the character's situation from good to bad or from bad to good. Reversals are what move a story forward. If only good things (or only bad things) happen to your character—or if everything they do works out just like they thought it would—the story isn't very exciting.

Think of a reversal as a "BUT THEN . . . " moment. The story is going one way for a while, BUT THEN something happens that causes the story to change direction. These can be small moments, such as this example, from Chapter 3:

- Tom gets a job offer! BUT THEN he finds out it'll never lead to the scientist job he really wants, so he turns it down. BUT THEN Dr. Palindrome lies to him, so Tom takes the job after all.

Or they can be really big moments:

- BUT THEN they accidentally travel back to the Stone Age! (More on that one soon!)

How do you put a reversal of fortune in your own story? One way is by doing what you just saw with Marisa. Your character thinks they're about to get what they want . . . BUT THEN something surprising happens, and they don't get it after all! This will be very disappointing, and they'll have to try something new to achieve their goal.

There are also lots of other kinds of reversals. Keep reading to see many more examples!

STORY CREATION ZONE

Write Like a Pro: Research vs. Making Stuff Up

When you write a story, you're creating a made-up world. You need to know enough about your world to make your audience feel like your setting could be real.

If you're writing a story about your own life, or a story with a setting that's similar to where you live, this isn't hard. Since you live in that world, you already know everything about it!

But if you're writing about a setting you've never been in yourself—like, say, a lab full of brilliant scientists or a prehistoric forest—it's much harder. You need to know enough details about your made-up setting to make your audience feel like it's real. But how can you come up with all those details?

You have two basic options:

First, you can use your **imagination** and just make everything up!

Second, you can do **research** about actual worlds like the ones you're writing about. For example, if you're writing about a scientist who just invented a new solar panel, you can go on the internet and search for stories about real solar panels. If you're writing about a world set in the Stone Age, you can read books about what experts think life was really like back then.

The best approach is usually a combination of these two: Do some research to learn more about your world, then use your imagination to fill in the gaps.

That's what Geoff Rodkey did when he wrote *Stuck in*

the Stone Age. For example, when Marisa introduces her amazing new solar panel invention, she says it's made from "graphene and molybdenum disulfide." These are real-life compounds that are used to make real-life solar panels, which Geoff learned by searching online for articles about solar panels. Does Geoff actually know how to build a solar panel? No way! He did enough research to make the solar panels seem real.

Even if you have an amazing imagination, a little research will help you make the most of it.

Science Fiction Zone: Mostly Made-Up Inventions

Just like its name says, science fiction is a mix of *science* and *fiction.* Adding some real science can help turbocharge your made-up fiction.

For example, in Chapter 2, Tom mentions the word *fluotanium* when he's talking about the *Star Trip* TV show. Is fluotanium real? Heck no!

BUT, there IS a real element called fluorine. And there's another real element called titanium.

Does Geoff Rodkey know anything about fluorine or titanium? Not really. But by mashing two real words together, he made up a fake word that sounds real. All it took was a little bit of research and some imagination. Look up "periodic table" online to find tons of science words you can mash up yourself!

Sometimes, the things in a science fiction story are so advanced that they're **mostly made-up**. Here are some common made-up inventions that show up again and again in sci-fi:

- Hyperdrives that let spaceships travel between stars
- Superintelligent robots
- Teleportation devices that send people or objects from one place to another instantly
- Aliens that can control your mind
- Machines or potions that give you superpowers
- Portals that let you travel to another dimension

Inventions like these are great in a sci-fi story. They might be something that *causes* a big problem, like our time machine will; they might help *solve* a big problem; or they might just be a cool vehicle your character drives.

Turn the page to see an example of a Mostly Made-Up Invention: the time machine from our story.

If you're writing a sci-fi story, you might want to use a Mostly Made-Up Invention Organizer of your own. If so, just grab some paper and draw one!

STORY CREATION ZONE

WHAT'S THE INVENTION CALLED?

Dr. Vasquez's Time Machine

WHAT DOES IT DO?

Travels through time

DRAW IT! LABEL IMPORTANT PARTS AND DESCRIBE WHAT THEY DO.

GREEN LEVER

· THE FETCHER ·
Use it to send the
machine through
a time with
no one in it.

DON'T GET
WET !!

🚜 Storytelling 101: We've Got a Problem!

Finally! We've reached the **main problem** of our story: Tom and Marisa have just accidentally transported themselves back to the Stone Age.

The main problem is the heart of a story's **plot**. Just like *protagonist* is a fancy word for "main character," *plot* is a fancy word for "everything that happens" in a story. The plot starts with whatever causes your character's problem and ends with whatever they finally do to solve (or fail to solve) it.

The moment a problem first appears is a major **reversal of fortune** that turns the story in a completely different direction. For Tom and Marisa, suddenly going from the present day to 10,000 B.C. changes the story completely.

If you're creating your own story, *any* problem you think is interesting for your character to try to solve can be a good one. Here are some ways you can brainstorm a main problem:

- **What Does the Character Want?** This is the simplest way to create the problem. Is your main character a basketball player who wants to win the big tournament? Or a flying hippopotamus on a quest to find a magical ice cream cone? Trying to win that tournament or find that ice cream cone is now their problem.

- **A Terrible Mistake Is Made:** The main character accidentally causes the problem by trying to get what they want. Is your character an astronaut who gets lost while on a mission to fly a spaceship to a new planet? Are they an absent-minded delivery person who accidentally lets a dinosaur loose in the city? Just a normal kid who makes their best friend extremely angry by saying the wrong thing in front of a group of other kids? These can be great problems, especially if the main character is responsible for causing them.

- **What's the Main Character's Weakness?** Sometimes you can imagine a good problem by looking at your character's weaknesses. If your character is terrified of children, what if they're forced to become a teacher? If your character has tons of energy and can't sit still for more than a minute, what if they get seated right behind the president during an important and incredibly long speech that millions of people are watching on TV?

- **What's the Main Character's Job?** If they're a firefighter, do they have to put out a huge fire? If they're a superhero, has a supervillain taken a whole city hostage? If they're a detective or a police officer, is there a crime they have to solve?

- **Something in the Setting Goes Wrong**: Take a look at your setting. Is there a problem that might be exciting to see there? Does an undiscovered volcano erupt in the middle of your main character's town? Does a tiger get loose at their local zoo? What if a new kid arrives in school and is just plain mean? Problems can come from anywhere.

Science Fiction Zone: Sci-Fi Problems

As we've said, science fiction stories are full of wild, strange, and amazing but true things (or at least, things that *might* be true someday). So the problems in sci-fi stories can get very weird:

- **A Mostly Made-Up Invention goes horribly wrong:** Does a spaceship break down in a dangerous place or accidentally travel hundreds of light-years in the wrong direction? Maybe a superintelligent robot goes haywire and becomes very dangerous. Or a scientist creates an invention that seems great but has terrible side effects.

- **Aliens come to Earth:** This is a classic one. There are tons of exciting problems that can happen when aliens come to Earth. Are the aliens unfriendly and try to mess up Earth? Or are they friendly, but the humans misunderstand them and try to make them go away? What if their only food is pencils, and suddenly there's a worldwide pencil shortage?

- **Humans go to a strange new world:** There are a lot of reasons humans might end up in a strange new world. Do they get trapped there and have to find a way home? Maybe their home is in trouble, and they're looking for a new place to live. And this strange new world can be anything from another planet to a totally different dimension.

- **Extreme disasters:** Some sci-fi stories take a real-life problem but make it extreme. There's a tornado coming, but it's a super tornado, the biggest ever seen! Or there's a volcano the size of Texas! What if the moon is exploding? Or Jupiter is crashing into the sun? To solve an extreme problem, your characters will probably need to find extreme solutions. They might even have to bring in a Mostly Made-Up Invention to save the day!

⛈️ Idea Storm: The Main Problem

What kind of problem do you want in your story?

- Do you want your main character to spend the whole story trying to get something they want?
- Do they make a mistake that causes a problem they didn't see coming?
- Does the problem hit them at a point of their greatest weakness?
- Does something bad happen in the setting, and they're forced to do something about it?

There's no wrong answer, and you definitely have PERMISSION TO GET WEIRD.

🏗️ Storytelling 101: Make Your Problem HUGE

We've almost finished the beginning of our story. We've met our **characters**, we know their **setting**, and most importantly, we know the **main problem** they're going to spend the rest of the story trying to solve: Tom and Marisa are stuck in the Stone Age.

Before we move on to the **middle** of our story, we need to do something fun for us but not so fun for our main characters: turn the **problem** into a **huge problem**. The bigger the problem seems and the harder it is to solve, the more your audience will be on the edge of their seats. They'll be eager to know what your characters will do to get themselves out of trouble.

In Tom and Marisa's case, just accidentally traveling back to the Stone Age would've been scary. But look at what happens in the first few minutes after they arrive:

- The green lever that should send them back to the present doesn't work.
- The time machine is on the edge of a cliff, and cavemen are trying to knock it off.
- Tom and Marisa have to jump out, or they'll be killed!
- They escape certain death, but when they try to get back to the time machine, it disappears!

Now Tom and Marisa don't just have a problem, they have a HUGE one: They're stranded in the Stone Age with no way to get back to the present. Not only that, but the cavemen who were trying to kill them are still running around!

When you're planning your story, sometimes it's

232

helpful to draw a chart like the one on page 235. It maps out how you'll crank up the tension by making your character's problem as hard to solve as possible.

How will our characters ever get out of this mess? As huge as their problem is, could it get EVEN WORSE? That's what we'll spend the **middle** of the story trying to figure out.

Idea Storm: Make Your Problem HUGE!

Try taking the problem in your story and making it HUGE. Think about how you can make it bigger, more threatening, and harder for your character to solve. It might help to grab some paper and draw a chart like the one on page 235. Here are some examples to get you started:

- **If your problem is that a volcano is erupting in your character's town** . . . Does their house catch on fire? Are they stranded in the middle of a ring of fire, cut off from their friends? Do lava monsters suddenly appear? (*Lava monsters*?! Why not? Remember to give yourself PERMISSION TO GET WEIRD.)

- **If your problem is that your characters want to win a basketball tournament** . . . Is there a reason why it's important to win the tournament? Is their family or their school counting on them to win a cash prize? What could make winning even harder? Does a rival team show up with a seven-foot-tall center? Is the rival team notorious for sneaky, underhanded fouls—and when the hero's team plays them, the referee gets something in her eye and can't call the fouls?

- **If your problem is that your character gets in a fight with their best friend** . . . What can make the fight worse or make it urgent that they find a way to make peace? Is the friend about to move away forever, so there won't be any time to make up? Does the fight happen on the day they're supposed to go on a long trip together?

No matter what your character's problem is, there are ways you can make it even bigger, more urgent, or harder to solve.

⭐ MAKE YOUR PROBLEM HUGE. ⭐

What's the problem? Use details!

Marisa accidentally sends the time machine back to 10,000 BC! Tom is stuck inside with her!

But it gets worse...

The time machine is on the edge of a cliff, and cavemen are about to roll a boulder down to knock it off. Tom and Marisa could DIE!

And even worse...

They have to jump out of the time machine, and it falls to the bottom of a cliff. If they don't get back in time, it will disappear.

You won't even believe how much worse it gets!

Tom almost drowns, and they don't get back fast enough. The time machine disappears! Now they're REALLY stuck in the Stone Age!

STORY CREATION ZONE

Write Like a Pro:
Pacing for Excitement

Go back and take a close look at the way Chapter 9 of *Stuck in the Stone Age* is written, especially the second half of it.

You might notice something.

Something about this chapter.

The sentences are very short.

There's quick, no-nonsense dialogue.

We're in suspense about each . . .

. . . exciting . . .

. . . MOMENT.

When you change the speed or rhythm of your writing, you're controlling the **pacing**. It's like when a movie goes into slow motion—or, the opposite, cuts between images in rapid-fire fashion, leaving the audience breathless with excitement. Instead of watching this happen on-screen, you're making it happen in the reader's mind by making the flow of words faster or slower.

When you write a scene with a lot of exciting action, pacing your writing will draw attention to each individual

STORY CREATION ZONE

moment and keep readers on the edge of their seats. For example, one sequence in this chapter could have just been written as:

Instead of answering, Marisa jumped off the cliff and landed safely in the water.

That's exactly what happened, but it's not exciting to read. Instead of writing it that way, Geoff Rodkey stretched the moment out. He let us feel the same "what's going to happen?" suspense that the characters are feeling:

Instead of answering, Marisa jumped off the cliff. Tom gasped.

An endless second later, she hit the water and disappeared.

"DR. MORICE?" Tom yelled.

Marisa's head bobbed up from below the surface, so far away it looked to Tom like it was the size of a pea.

This makes the scene much more fun to read, because it keeps the reader guessing about what's coming next.

You can use this in your own writing! Control the pacing of an action scene by following these tips:

- Focus on exactly what the characters are doing in each moment. Describe action.
- Don't give everything away all at once. Take it one thing at a time. Keep your reader in . . .
- Suspense!

- Mix in dialogue with the action. If your characters are frightened or excited, make them sound that way by speaking in short bursts, with a lot of emphasis. "You know! Like *THIS*!"

- Imagine YOU are the character experiencing that moment. Would your heart be racing? Would you feel like you want to throw up? Let your audience know what your characters are feeling and thinking.

- *CRASH!* Sound effects can be exciting.

THE MIDDLE

Now that we've got a character with a problem, things are really heating up. We're in the MIDDLE of the story!

Storytelling 101: Obstacles

In the **middle** of the story, our characters try to solve their **problem** (which is now HUGE), but we can't make it too easy for them. If they solve the problem right away, it's not much of a problem—and not much of a story, either. Here's an example:

The Pirate Who Wanted Some Cheese

Once upon a time, there was a pirate who wanted some cheese. But there was NO CHEESE ANYWHERE IN THE WORLD!! "OH, no!! What a huge problem!" he screamed.

Then the pirate noticed some cheese right next to him on the counter. "Oh. There's some cheese. My mistake."

The End

Your story will be much more interesting if you make the problem very hard to solve.

One way to do this is to create **obstacles**. Obstacles are the smaller problems that your character has to solve before being able to tackle the main problem.

If you play video games, you run into these problem-within-a-problem obstacles all the time. Say you're playing a game where your goal is to save the kingdom from a dragon. You set out to find the dragon, but then you come to a river, and its bridge has collapsed! You can't get back to tracking down the dragon until you figure out how to cross the river. That missing bridge is an obstacle—and you'll probably run into a lot of those before you even reach the big dragon battle.

In Chapters 10 and 11 of *Stuck in the Stone Age*, Tom and Marisa face several obstacles, each one bigger than the last. Here they are in and Obstacle Organizer:

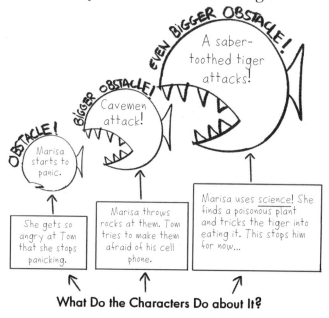

What Do the Characters Do about It?

The first obstacle, Marisa's panic attack, is pretty minor. The second obstacle is the attack by the cavemen. That's much bigger and more urgent. If Tom and Marisa don't solve that, they could die! Tom tries to use his phone to frighten the cavemen away, but it doesn't seem like that's going to work—until the cavemen suddenly run away! What a **reversal of fortune**! Except it turns out they only left because of . . .

The third obstacle: A saber-toothed tiger shows up and

tries to eat them! This is the most serious obstacle of all. Fortunately, in yet another reversal, Marisa overcomes the life-threatening obstacle (for now) by poisoning the tiger.

There's no wrong way to get past an obstacle. In fact, your characters might find totally different solutions to the exact same obstacles. It's important to think about how their **strengths** and **weaknesses** give them ideas for what to do. For example, Marisa's great strength, her scientific knowledge, is what saves their lives when she spots the poisonous berries. When your characters use their strengths and weaknesses to deal with obstacles, it makes them seem more realistic and more interesting.

Idea Storm: Obstacles

Now you try it! Think about some obstacles that might get in the way while your character is trying to deal with the **main problem**. How is each obstacle handled? Does the character solve it using one of their strengths? Do their weaknesses lead them to a bad or goofy solution? Worse, do their weaknesses cause the obstacle or make it worse?

Grab some paper and draw your own Obstacle Organizer!

🏗️ Storytelling 101: Villain Check-In

When we last discussed Dr. Palindrome, we weren't sure he was a villain. But now we've seen him erase the only evidence that Tom and Marisa are stuck in the Stone Age—making their **main problem** much harder to solve! It's clear that Dr. Palindrome is a bad guy.

But he isn't the only villain in this story. The saber-toothed tiger (who we'll learn is named Tooka) wants to eat Tom and Marisa! A **villain** is someone who stands in the main character's way, trying to stop them from getting what they want or solving their problem. And eating them would definitely get in their way. So it's safe to say that Tooka is a villain.

What about the cavemen? They've thrown rocks at Tom and Marisa twice already, so they *seem* like villains. We don't know enough about them yet to be sure that they won't become **shape-shifter** characters, who start out as villains and later turn into **allies** of our main characters. We'll have to wait and see.

If you have a story with a villain (or villains) in it, it's helpful to keep track of both *how* they're trying to stop the main character and *why* they're doing it. A good villain always **wants** something (just like a main character wants something), which is what puts them in conflict with the main character.

Check out the Villain Organizer we used to track the villains in *Stuck in the Stone Age*. If your story has a villain, you might want to use one of these, too!

☠ VILLAIN! ☠

Who is the villain?	How will they stop the main characters from getting what they want?	Why are they doing it? (What do they want?)
Dr. Palindrome—the scientist in charge of CEASE	By erasing the evidence that Tom and Marisa are stuck in the Stone Age and by trying to take credit for inventing Marisa's solar panels	Fame and money
Who is the villain?	**How will they stop the main characters from getting what they want?**	**Why are they doing it? (What do they want?)**
Tooka the saber-toothed tiger	By eating them	Eating humans is fun, and Tom and Marisa smell tasty. Plus, they woke him up, so he is grumpy.

⛈ Idea Storm: Villains

Does your story have a villain—a character who's going to try to stop your main character from solving their problem and getting what they want?

Not all stories do. Sometimes, what's keeping the character from getting what they want is just their situation—perhaps an avalanche, an illness, or not having enough money to get something they need. Sometimes, the main character is standing in their own way. Maybe they have a weakness, like a short temper, that causes their problem.

If your story has a villain, the more you know about them, the better your story will be. You can draw your own Villain Organizer to get you started. Or, if you want to go even more in depth with your villain, you can draw a whole Character Creator to ask the same questions about your villain that you do about your main character: What are the villain's strengths? What are their weaknesses? Have fun with it, and don't be afraid to GET WEIRD!

Write Like a Pro: The ~~Five~~ SIX! Senses of Setting

To make your readers feel like your story's actually happening and that they're right in the middle of the action, it helps to think about the **setting** from your **main character**'s senses. When they first enter a new setting, what does it look like? Feel like? Sound like? Even taste and smell like?

The more you can use the five senses—sight, hearing,

smell, taste, and touch—to add details, the more your setting will come alive.

At the Story Pirates, we like to add a sixth sense: a **sense of danger**!

Most people don't include danger with the other five senses. But we do! Because if you think about it, every interesting setting has some kind of danger. It's not always physical danger, but a sense that something could go wrong at any time.

If your setting is a school, that sixth sense might be your main character's fear of not making friends. If it's a basketball court, the danger is that the other team could win. If it's a pancake factory, there could be a team of ninjas lurking in the shadows!

The scene in Chapter 14 of *Stuck in the Stone Age*, when Tom and Marisa arrive at Dug's cave, is a good example of writing with all six senses. There's the *sight* of flickering firelight. The *sound* of cavepeople shrieking in fear. The *smell* of sewage, body odor, and dead animals. The *taste* of berries and nuts. The *feel* of getting smacked in the head by low-flying bat wings. And the *danger* of not just an obvious, in-your-face threat (a caveman who tries to attack them with a club), but unseen and longer-term threats (the diseases they could catch from the sewage, and the tiger they know is still lurking in the darkness outside the cave).

Thinking about all six senses can also help you write by **showing, not telling**. Once you've thought about all these sense details, show how they make your characters feel and what they *do* as a result.

For example, in *Stuck in the Stone Age*, we learn that the cave smells pretty bad, but the setting comes to life when we see Tom's reaction:

> *It was like a combination of sewage, body odor, and dead animals.*
>
> *But mostly sewage.*
>
> *"Oh, geez," said Tom, putting his hands in front of his nose. "That's powerful stuff."*

It's pretty amazing that Tom manages to smell all that stuff without throwing up!

Storytelling 101: A Big Twist!

Holy cow! The cavepeople don't just fear Tooka the tiger, they worship him! And they make human sacrifices to him! And now they've just sacrificed Marisa to him! How will she ever get out of this?!

That's a heck of a **plot twist**! A twist is just like a **reversal of fortune**, except it's usually a HUGE SURPRISE both to the audience and the story's characters (some of them, anyway). A twist makes your audience feel like they're on a roller coaster that just made a hairpin turn, and they have no idea what will happen next.

Sometimes, the twist makes the **problem** much bigger or more urgent.

Sometimes, the twist involves a **shape-shifter** character who we suddenly realize is a **villain**.

Sometimes, the twist reveals that everything the **main character** was doing to solve their problem was actually making it worse. Or it reveals that they were trying to solve the wrong problem, and the REAL problem is something completely different.

And sometimes, there's no big twist at all! Not every story has to have one.

Write Like a Pro: Show BEFORE You Tell

One key to creating a great plot twist is to "show BEFORE you tell," or "plant it early and pay it off later."

In other words, you should set up a small **clue** early

in the story. But make it small enough that the reader won't notice until it pays off when the big twist arrives.

For example, in *Stuck in the Stone Age*, we first learn about the big sacrificial pit in Chapter 14:

"Look out!"

It was a three-foot-wide, ten-foot-deep pit about twenty yards in front of the cave entrance.

"What do you think that's for?" Tom asked.

Marisa shrugged. "Self-defense?"

When you read that, you probably thought, "What's up with that pit?" It was a mystery to the audience and to Marisa and Tom, as well. When the characters stopped talking about it, you probably stopped thinking about it, too. That is, until a few chapters later, when Dug tossed Marisa into the pit, and its purpose was revealed in the big twist.

That early clue is important, because if we don't learn about the pit until right before Dug tosses Marisa into it, the moment might feel a little fake. But if we've known for a while that the pit is there, it's much more believable (and satisfying) when the big twist arrives and we learn the pit's true purpose.

Idea Storm: Twists and Reversals

Want to put a big twist in your story? We can help!

Start by looking at your setting. Remember the sixth sense of danger we talked about? Think of something dangerous in your setting that will make your character's main problem or one of their **obstacles** harder to solve.

But then, keep that danger a secret from the main characters—and the reader. Just plant a clue early in the story, which they'll remember when the twist happens later.

Here are some examples to help you brainstorm:

- There's a locked door in the basement. What's on the other side? A secret treasure? A spy who's been kidnapped? If it's a treasure, did your character hear a rumor about it early on in the story? If it's a spy, did your character hear mysterious yelling at some point?

- Your basketball team's headed for the finals of the big tournament! But when you all get on the bus to leave for the game, the bus breaks down! Suddenly, that strange clicking noise that the engine made when you drove to the semifinal game seems a lot more meaningful.

- That robot butler sure is neat—polite, helpful,

and quiet—which makes it very surprising when the robot suddenly ties up your main character and steals their car!

Here's an important thing to keep in mind when you're putting a big twist into your story: If you've already started writing, you'll probably have to go back and put a clue into an earlier part of the story. That early clue about the pit didn't appear in Geoff Rodkey's first draft of Chapter 14. He had to go back and add it later once he decided the pit would be important in Chapter 19. It's like we said at the beginning: All the best writing comes from RE-writing things!

🏗️ Storytelling 101: Trying! Failing. Trying Again!

Hurray! In Chapter 20, Marisa finally got past her most life-threatening **obstacle**: Tooka the saber-toothed tiger. This obstacle was so big that she wasn't able to solve it right away. She had to try (and fail) several times before she finally succeeded. Take a look at the next page.

Having your character try and fail to solve a problem is a great way to create the **reversals of fortune** that make your story exciting to read. It can also make their obstacle

☠️ SOLVE THE PROBLEM ☠️

WHAT IS THE PROBLEM?
Tooka the saber-toothed tiger wants to eat Marisa and Tom.

THE **FIRST** THING MY CHARACTER TRIES:

Marisa finds a poisonous plant and puts it in a sandwich for Tooka to eat.

UNFORTUNATELY... (WHAT WENT WRONG?)

It only makes him sick for a few days. Now he is <u>angry</u>.

THE **NEXT** THING MY CHARACTER TRIES:

She tries to build a tiger trap by putting lots of pointy sticks in the bottom of a pit.

UNFORTUNATELY... (WHAT WENT WRONG?)

No one will help her, and it's too much work to do alone. Plus, the cave people don't want it to be a tiger trap anyway. Secretly, they want it to be a <u>human</u> trap to offer Tooka food.

THE SOLUTION THAT **FINALLY** WORKS:

She gets thrown in the pit, but finds a big pointy stick, which she sets up so Tooka will land on it.

THIS WORKS BECAUSE:

Tooka thinks Marisa is no match for him, so he jumps right in the pit and onto the pointy stick. Bye-bye, Tooka.

251

or problem even worse. For example, when Marisa made Tooka sick by feeding him the poisoned berries, he became even angrier and more determined to eat her.

In some shorter stories, having a character try several times to solve a problem (and finally succeed) takes up the entire **middle** section. Then you're already at the end of the story! If you ever have to write a story for school, or if you're just in the mood to write a short story of your own, the Solve the Problem Organizer can be your secret weapon. Think of a character and a problem, and then use the organizer to plan the middle of your story. Easy!

Unfortunately for Marisa, she hasn't made it to the end yet. She still has to solve her main problem and find a way out of the Stone Age. At least now she can breathe a sigh of relief, knowing she won't have to worry about Tooka anymore. Things should be easier from now on, right?

Well, not necessarily. Remember that stories are full of reversals of fortune. A moment like this one, when the character has tried and tried to solve a problem, and finally succeeded—at just the moment when they're feeling most awesome about themselves—can be a very exciting time for the writer to have something HUGE go wrong. Keep reading and we'll show you what we mean.

⚒ Storytelling 101: The Darkest Hour

We're almost done with the middle section of the story—and that means bad news for the main characters. This is because, in the same way that the beginning ends with the characters realizing what their **huge problem** is, the middle ends with them facing their **darkest hour**. In other words, things are about to get *really* bad for the main characters, so bad that they almost lose hope completely.

For example, just seconds after her big success in defeating Tooka, Dug is furious that Marisa's just killed the tiger his tribe worships. He suddenly decides to kill *her*. Now things are even worse than before! What a huge **reversal of fortune**!

To top it off, both Tom and Marisa are now sure they'll never get what they want. All Marisa ever wanted was to make friends, but now she's hiding alone in a cave with bats. All Tom ever wanted was to become a scientist, but Marisa has revealed to him that it won't ever happen. Their dreams are crushed, and they're furious with each other.

Wait a minute! This is awful! We want to go back to Tom and Marisa being friends and hoping that they find a way back from the Stone Age! Why would you ever want your characters to be this sad and hopeless?

253

Not to spoil anything, but the end of the story is coming up soon, and they probably *will* solve their big problem. BUT it's going to be much more exciting to watch them do it if you first pile up so much trouble for them that they will be convinced they'll never succeed.

Idea Storm: The Darkest Hour

Is your main character getting close to solving their main problem? Don't let them solve it too quickly! Before they finally succeed, give them a HUGE reversal of fortune: a darkest hour where it seems like everything is going wrong and they may never get what they want.

The real key to making this work is to make sure the reader understands *exactly* how terrible your characters feel in their darkest hour. One great way to do this is by using **words with flavor**. This is vocabulary that shows the audience *exactly* how someone feels.

Emotions are like colors. For every primary color like blue, there are LOTS of variations: navy, indigo, azure, cobalt, sapphire, cyan, turquoise, royal blue, baby blue . . . The list is almost endless.

For example, when Marisa loses control and finally tells Tom the truth about his job, the author doesn't say

"Marisa felt sad and mad." Here's how he describes it:

"You're not a scientist, Tom," she said in a bitter, seething voice.

Bitter! Seething! Those words really pack some punch! Here are a few more words with flavor.

Different flavors of "sad"	Different flavors of "mad"	Different flavors of "mad" and "sad" at the same time (and probably a little mean)
blue	peeved	bitter
despondent	irritated	petulant
gloomy	enraged	resentful
heartbroken	fuming	spiteful
melancholy	furious	sulky
pessimistic	infuriated	sullen
somber	irate	vengeful
sorrowful	outraged	
	seething	
	wrathful	

If you're looking for even more words with flavor, try looking in a thesaurus. A thesaurus is a book or online database that has lists of similar but very specific words you can use for any situation. Just make sure that if you choose an unfamiliar word from a thesaurus, you look it up first in a dictionary. You want to be certain that the word means exactly what you want it to mean.

THE END

 Just when it seems like all is lost, we reach THE ENDING. It's when all the hard work pays off for your character, your audience, and YOU the writer!

Storytelling 101: The Climax!

Finally! Tom and Marisa have made it back to the present day! This is the story's **climax**—the moment when the characters finally solve their problem.

It isn't easy. It shouldn't be! The harder your main character has to work to solve the problem, the more satisfying your story will be.

For example, it would have been a real letdown if Chapter 27 of *Stuck in the Stone Age* just went like this:

Marisa and Tom saw the fetcher. They got it from the lake. They pressed the button and went back to their own time.

That isn't fun to read at all! Luckily for the reader, it's not that simple. Getting the fetcher back is hard, and our characters need to come up with a plan to make it happen. And then, they face a bunch of obstacles and reversals before they finally get back to their own time.

As usual, there's no wrong way for the characters to

get past the obstacles, but it can help to think about their **strengths** and **weaknesses**.

Because this story has two main characters, they can team up and combine their strengths to solve the problem. It takes Marisa's science knowledge to both build the crane and create the explosives they use to trick the cavepeople. And it takes Tom's people skills to manage the cavemen when they're operating the crane to fish the fetcher out of the lake.

In stories with just one main character, they often have to overcome their big weakness to solve the problem. For example, if Tom had been alone in the Stone Age, he would've had to get the fetcher out of the water without Marisa's knowledge to help him.

It's a lot of fun to watch a character finally overcome their weakness. For example, Marisa was too shy to correct either Dr. Palindrome or the cavemen when they kept getting her name wrong in the beginning and middle of the story. Finally, at the end of Chapter 26, she gets the courage to correct them:

"MY ... NAME ... IS ... MARISA!"

Seeing Marisa find the courage to overcome her weakness of being shy and nervous is pretty awesome!

⛈️ Idea Storm: Plan the Climax

Does your main character solve their big problem? Whether they do or not, make sure your story's **climax** takes into account the main character's strengths and weaknesses. If they solve the problem, they should do it using their strengths—either the same strengths they've shown since the beginning of the story OR weaknesses that they've overcome.

Try not to make the solution too easy. It's much more satisfying if your main character really has to dig deep. The more reversals and obstacles you can add as they pursue the solution, the better.

Check out the Plan the Climax Organizer we made for Tom and Marisa. You can draw your own to map out exactly how your characters put their plan into action—and what obstacles get in their way.

Don't be afraid to rewrite your climax if you think of a more challenging way to solve your character's problem. The ending is often the hardest part of a story to write. Many writers change the climax more than once before they find the right one for their story.

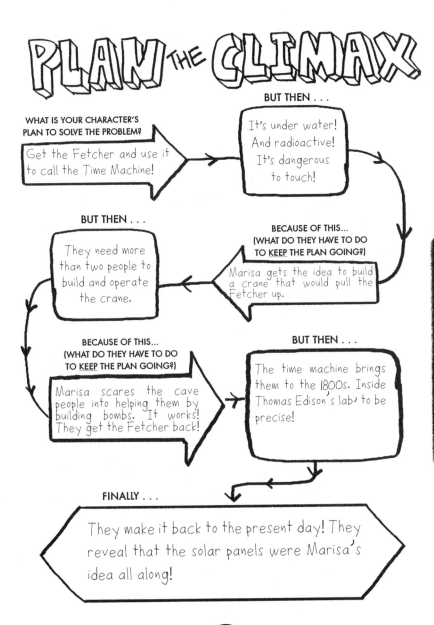

PLAN THE CLIMAX

WHAT IS YOUR CHARACTER'S PLAN TO SOLVE THE PROBLEM?

Get the Fetcher and use it to call the Time Machine!

BUT THEN . . .

It's under water! And radioactive! It's dangerous to touch!

BECAUSE OF THIS... (WHAT DO THEY HAVE TO DO TO KEEP THE PLAN GOING?)

Marisa gets the idea to build a crane that would pull the Fetcher up.

BUT THEN . . .

They need more than two people to build and operate the crane.

BECAUSE OF THIS... (WHAT DO THEY HAVE TO DO TO KEEP THE PLAN GOING?)

Marisa scares the cave people into helping them by building bombs. It works! They get the Fetcher back!

BUT THEN . . .

The time machine brings them to the 1800s. Inside Thomas Edison's lab, to be precise!

FINALLY . . .

They make it back to the present day! They reveal that the solar panels were Marisa's idea all along!

STORY CREATION ZONE

📷 Storytelling 101: Getting What They Want . . . In a Surprising Way

Once we've reached the story's **climax**, and the **huge problem** has been solved, is the story over?

You actually have at least one more interesting decision to make: What kind of ending do you want for your story? How will the story look after the problem has finally been solved? You have a few options:

- **To Be Continued:** Right when we think everything is wrapped up, the characters run into a new problem! But there's no time left in the story to solve it, so the reader is left wondering what happens next. (Like how Dr. Palindrome escapes in the time machine!)

- **Happily Ever After:** The classic way to finish is with a Happily Ever After ending. Tom and Marisa make it back, Dr. Palindrome gets fired and swears to never be a villain again, and all the other scientists are friends forever.

- **The Tragic Ending:** This is the opposite of Happily Ever After. Marisa gets eaten by Tooka, Tom is stuck in the Stone Age forever, and Dr. Palindrome gets rich and famous. Certain readers will get angry that you wrote something so sad, but other readers will love you for it. (Some people get tired of all those Happily Ever After endings)

- **The "Twist" Ending**: Sometimes the **twist** in a story happens right at the end, when you least expect it. Dr. Palindrome reveals that he's actually . . . Marisa's long-lost father! Keeping her stuck in the Stone Age was just his weird plan to help her overcome her fears and build confidence! (That example is obviously a little silly, but the twist can be anything—*except* having the whole story be a dream, where the main character wakes up safe in bed. Don't do that one. It's been done so often at this point, it's not even a twist anymore.)

Because Tom and Marisa solve their main problem, *Stuck in the Stone Age* has a happy ending. Most comedies have a happy ending, because they're usually meant to make the audience feel good. On the other hand, it's not exactly a "Happily Ever After" ending. It's something a little more interesting. Let's call it a "**Characters Get What They Want . . . In a Surprising Way**" ending. Here's what we mean.

Tom always wanted to be a scientist, but in the **darkest hour**, Marisa tells him he'll never be one. After thinking it over, he realizes she's right. He can't get what he wants after all.

In Marisa's case, she wanted to not be lonely, and she tried to achieve that goal by making an invention so awesome that everyone would love her. But when she comes back to the present and finds herself surrounded by reporters asking questions, she realizes she doesn't want to be around *too* many people. What she really wants is one really good friend.

So Tom can't get what he wants, while Marisa realizes she doesn't want what she thought she wanted. That sounds like a less-than-happy ending. But there's one more **reversal** left in the story.

When Tom loses his job and Marisa quits CEASE to start her new solar panel company, Marisa has the brilliant idea to ask Tom to be the spokesman for her new company. It's the perfect solution! Not only will Tom get to be around the science he loves so much, but the job fits his big **strength**, which is getting along with people. By going into business with Tom, Marisa won't be lonely anymore—they'll get to have lunch together every day! But she will be able to spend most of her time alone, working on the science that's her big strength.

In the end, they both get what they want, but not in

the way they (or the audience) expected.

They've also learned something about themselves. Tom learned that he really isn't very good at science. Marisa learned that she's actually an introvert who doesn't want to be around people as much as she thought.

In the end, Tom and Marisa have changed. They both end up happier and more aware of their own strengths and weaknesses than when the story started. When characters change like this over the course of a story, it's called a **character arc**.

Idea Storm: Did Your Character Change, Grow, or Learn?

What kind of ending do you want to have in your story? Happy? Sad? Something weird or in between? It's up to you to decide what works best for *your* story.

Now look back at your story and your main character's journey through it. Does your character have an arc? In other words, do things happen in the story that cause them to change? Does their life get better? Worse? Do they learn something about themselves or about the world? Do they become more (or less) kind, helpful, friendly, or generous?

It's okay if they don't change! In some stories, especially action stories, the main character is pretty much exactly the same at the end of the story as they were at the beginning.

But having your main character learn, grow, or change over the course of your story is a great way to give the story a bigger emotional impact—for your characters, for your audience, and for you as a writer.

This is the last of the Idea Storms. Did you do them all? If so . . .

CONGRATULATIONS! YOU JUST WROTE A STORY!

Take a look back at your Idea Storms. If you did them all, you:

- Created a character
- Established a setting
- Gave your character a main problem
- Made the problem HUGE
- Put some obstacles in your character's way
- Revealed your story's villain
- Plotted some twists and reversals

- Plunged your character into their darkest hour
- Brought them back from the brink to solve the problem in the climax, and
- Showed how solving the problem gave your character an arc of growth, learning, or change

That's a whole story. You did it! Wow! Amazing job! You're officially a writer!

So now what?

Go back and make it better! Remember how we said that all the best writing comes from RE-writing things? It's true! Go rewrite the weak parts! Make the huge problem even more huge! Make the twist even twist-ier by turning your main character's best friend into a shape-shifting villain! Don't be afraid to cross things out and get messy!

OR . . .

Start a brand-new story! Give yourself permission to make this one EVEN MORE WEIRD!

OR . . .

Just go eat a cookie. You deserve it! You wrote a whole story! Congrats again! You are awesome.

APPENDIX:
Vince's Original Idea (With Spoilers!)

Here's the complete idea that Vince originally submitted for *Stuck in the Stone Age.*

But if you haven't read the whole story yet, ARE YOU SURE YOU WANT TO READ THIS? Because there are spoilers. Don't say we didn't warn you. It's not too late to turn back!

Okay, here it is.

THE SPARK: WHAT SHOULD THIS BOOK BE ABOUT?

NAME OF MAIN CHARACTER:

Dr. Tom Edison and Dr. Morice

DESCRIBE THE MAIN CHARACTER:

They are both stuck in the past full of cavemen because they teleported in a fellow scientist's time machine (the time machine was unsteady). They are also both chemical reaction scientists.

IS THERE SOMETHING THE MAIN CHARACTER WANTS MORE THAN ANYTHING IN THE WORLD . . . OR . . . DOES THE MAIN CHARACTER HAVE A PROBLEM THEY'RE TRYING TO SOLVE?

The scientists need to get back to their time because a saber tooth tiger was hunting them.

WHAT (OR WHO) IS PREVENTING THE MAIN CHARACTER FROM GETTING WHAT THEY WANT AND/OR SOLVING THE PROBLEM?
The time machine is gone, it teleported back to the right time. They accidentally fall into a radioactive lake and teleport back through time to their time.

ARE THERE ANY OTHER DETAILS ABOUT THE STORY THAT YOU WANT US TO KNOW?

Dr. Morice is always down on things and Tom knows everything about Star Wars and Star Trek.

CEO: Benjamin Salka
Artistic Director: Lee Overtree
Education Director: Quinton Johnson
Story Pirates Senior Management: Duke Doyle, Nicole Brodeur,
Peter McNerney, Jeremy Basescu, Joanna Simmons, Sam Reiff-
Pasarew, Lauren Stripling, Graeme Hinde, Sherry Layne, Will
Kellogg, Jason Boxer, and Amanda Borson

ACKNOWLEDGMENTS

We would like to especially acknowledge our Education Director
Quinton Johnson, whose brilliant pedagogies underlie the Story
Creation Zone and without whom the Story Pirates would not be
teaching creative writing in such a dynamic, engaging, and
effective way.

We would also like to thank the following friends, colleagues,
and champions (in no particular order): Stephen Barbara, Rhea
Lyons, Derek Evans, Charlie Russo, Sam Forman, Adrienne
Becker, Laura Heywood, Allen Hubby, Eric Cipra, Jon Glickman,
Natalie Tucker, Gimlet Media, The Drama Book Shop, Maggie
Pisacane, Mark Merriman, Marcie Cleary, Mara Canner, Matt
Gehring, Brandon York, Eli Bolin, Bekah Nutt, Gabe Jewell,
Connor White, Annabeth Bondor-Stone, Amy Gargan, Lynn
Weingarten, and the hundreds of thousands of kids who have
sent us their stories since 2004.